# PISTOL PACKIN' MAMA

"I still say we should ride up there tonight, blow them guards away from that damn sluice gate and blast it to hell!" Westcheski shouted. He turned to the other men in the saloon.

"Any of you guys with me? Who wants to get some powder and go up the river and blow up that damn sluice gate? Just dynamite it into Lincoln County!"

A dozen liquored voices rang out in the affirmative. Spur knew the group; more important to him was Cain Haworth's reaction.

Cain pushed his chair back slowly, stood, adjusted his six-gun and walked toward the three men at the table.

"I'll go," he said. "I'll even show you where it is —then I'll blow your goddamn brains out!" Before any of the three could move, Cain's six-gun flashed into his hand and covered them.

"Now, what was all this big talk about blowing up something?"

The men looked at each other. At last Westcheski pushed his chair back, stood and started to turn, then threw the chair with surprising speed at the gunman. The heavy chair caught Cain on the side. It staggered him, but he kept his feet and the gun.

Spur didn't see her move, but all at once Claudine was behind Cain with a two-barreled .45 derringer in his back.

"No gunplay in here, Cain," she said. "I can put both slugs right through your spine before you can get a shot off, and you'll be dead before you beak in half."

SPUR #7

# MONTANA MINX

## DIRK FLETCHER

LEISURE BOOKS  NEW YORK CITY

A LEISURE BOOK®

December 2003

Published by

Dorchester Publishing Co., Inc.
200 Madison Avenue
New York, NY 10016

ISBN 0-8439-2177-3

Visit us on the web at www.dorchesterpub.com.

# Chapter One

July 22, 1873—East of Helena, Montana Territory.

*(In January, 1873, the great Credit Mobilier scandal was investigated by Congress and the swindle unearthed shamed many of the builders of the transcontinental railroad. Ulysses S. Grant was in his second year of his second term as President of the United States, with William M. Evarts as his Secretary of State, Henry Wilson his Vice President, and William K. Belknap was Secretary of War. Grant had won the election for a second term with 3,587,070 votes, beating out the famous "Go west young man, go west," Horace Greeley, a Democrat who gathered 2,834,079. This was the year the earmuff was invented by Chester Greenwood. The first formal list of rules for a new sport called "football" were put together in New York City in 1873.)*

The daily stage from Helena to High Prairie rolled along through the valley moving east and was now little less than an hour from its destination. The four passengers inside the sturdy but uncomfortable coach were hot and a fine sheen of dust had settled on everyone and everything.

The tall man who had slept most of the way was a drummer, his line of fine workingman's hand tools packed safely in his carpetbag in the boot. He was forty-two years old, had a thin face and a wife and three children in St. Louis. This was the end of his twice yearly swing through the "sticks" as he called the wilds of Montana. It had been a hard ride, and he admired the young woman who sat beside him. But he had said no more than a polite hello to her.

The woman was twenty-four, more starkly striking than pretty, slender and well dressed. She had slept part way leaning on a pillow she had brought against the side of the coach. She tugged at her dress which was sticking to her thighs. She was conscious of a drop of sweat rolling down her open necked dress and seeping into the line of cleavage just out of sight under the garment. Another hour and she would have a bath.

The seat opposite her held a matron of thirty-two and her ten-year-old son. The boy had been half out the window a dozen times and wanted to ride on top with the shotgun guard, but he had been told company regulations made that impossible. He was brown haired and full of energy. His mother leaned back and closed her eyes, hoping her husband would be at High Prairie to meet

6

her. He said the ranchhouse was ready to move into.

On the high seat at the front of the stage, George held the twelve reins in his practiced hands. He had been on this run for so long he knew every rock and rut. It hadn't rained for two months and the ruts were gone, filled in with sand and dirt and knocked flat by the pounding of twenty-four hooves a trip and the wide iron flat rims on the wooden spoked wheels.

They would be in town in less than an hour. The horses were in good shape. This was a quick easy run, the last day from Helena.

On the wooden bench beside him Will Manson checked the Spencer rifle he carried. He had only used it once on this run, and had driven off two attackers. He got a ten dollar bonus that day! It was as much as a whole week's pay and he had bought a new gold watch. He was just over fifty, and looking forward to quitting the guard job. Maybe next year. He squinted down the track of a roadway at the Peter's Creek crossing. It was a small ford that crossed to get on the right side before the river became so big down-stream they couldn't ford it. The area was always green because of the springs that fed the little creek, and the downstream flow.

This had been a favorite spot for a quick stop on days when they were ahead of schedule. Today they would swing right through, since they all were anxious to get into town.

The coach drew closer to the ford. George peered into the darkness under the trees, shadowed despite the hot sun. He could see nothing. Almost never anything to see.

They were thirty yards from the trees. Will Manson pulled down on the team of six to ease them to a walk through the foot deep water of the stream when they came to it. Not that much water today, George figured as he looked at the stream.

The first shot cracked through the silent Montana air with the surprise of a lightning bolt on a cloudless day.

George knew it was a Sharps when he heard the sound almost at the same time that a mighty fist pounded into his upper chest and sprawled him back over the top of the coach. His shoulder wedged against the little railing and his left hand grabbed it to keep from tumbling to the ground.

By that time there were a dozen shots blasting into the soft summer day. George saw Will slap the reins down on the six horses to get back up to speed. But another volley of shots came followed by a voice.

"Hold it! Stop the stage or you're all dead. We've got rifles, repeating rifles!"

Will Manson had wanted to make a run for it with the stage. But he knew better. Company policy was to run only when he would have a good chance to outdistance one or two gunmen. He had no clue how many guns were in the darkness ahead. He eased the rig to a stop just as it entered the shade twenty yards this side of the water.

Two masked men rode out of the brush on one side and two more from the other side. All carried rifles and holstered six-guns. There was little he could tell by the horses. No brands showed, which wasn't unusual.

A tall, thin man with a high-crowned black hat and a red bandana kerchief over his nose and mouth rode up to the coach while the others trained their rifles on the stage.

"Down!" he ordered in a whining voice.

Will helped his wounded shotgun guard down to the ground. The shoulder was bleeding badly.

"Can I stop the bleeding?" Will asked the robber.

"Hell, if you can." The tall rider motioned his rifle toward the stage doors. "Everybody out! No problems, or you eat rifle slugs for supper. Get out of there!"

The dummer came first, handing the two women down. The little boy jumped out and walked up to the robber.

"You an outlaw?" the boy asked.

"Jason!" his mother blurted. "Get back over here by me."

The robber tipped the brim of his hat. "All right, ma'am. Lad is curious. I used to be that way." He looked down at the boy. "I guess you could say I'm an outlaw, kid. Now you help. You get the ladies' reticules and the

9

man's wallet and his watch and all the rings and bring them to me."

"Yes sir!" Jason said grinning. He ran to his mother, took her reticule and stopped in front of the younger woman. By the time he had the purses and wallet, the tall robber had stepped off his horse. Two men had worked over the stage and shouted a moment later when they found a strong box in the boot at the rear covered by a blanket and an old canvas.

The leader bent down to take the reticules. Without any warning Jason's hand darted out, grabbed the mask and pulled it down, revealing a lean jaw, a hard mouth and broken nose. A thin scar showed on the right cheek through a day's beard. The robber jerked the mask up again, but it was too late.

"Goddamn, you're Cain Haworth!" Will Manson shouted. "I see you all the time in Prairie City."

Cain jolted his face up and stared at Manson. The stage driver grabbed his hat and slammed it against his leg. Too late he realized. The mistake he had made.

"No, no, not so," Manson said trying to undo the damage. "Can't be Cain at all, don't look nothing like him. Some other jasper. Ain't never seen this man before in my life."

Cain dropped the purses and leveled his six-gun at the stage driver.

"That was a bad mistake, driver. A damn fatal mistake. You know what we got to do now, don't you?"

"Christ! Six of us? You can't do that. Swear to God nobody will have any idea who robbed us. Shit, you can't just shoot six people. Women . . . two of them are women and the kid!"

Cain pulled the trigger and a small black hole appeared in Manson's forehead and almost at the same time a gush of blood, bone fragments and brain tissue splattered the side of the stage coach behind him. The body bounced off the coach and crumpled to the ground.

"Damnit, no!" one of the mounted men shouted. "Think what you're doing!"

Cain turned. "I am. You ain't the one identified, so shut up your ugly mouth!"

He had turned away for a moment, but it was enough time for the wounded shotgun guard to grab a derringer from his boot and pull the trigger twice. Two .41 caliber slugs whistled past Cain and caught the rider behind him in the chest. He toppled from his horse dead as he hit the dirt of the trail.

Cain turned and screamed, then shot George in the chest four times with his six-gun. His eyes were glaring, furious. A streak of spittle drooled from the corner of his mouth. After he shot the man he ran to him and stomped his face into a mass of blood and smashed bones until the shotgun guard was unrecognizable.

He whirled on the passengers who were still lined up near the stage. The drummer shivered. He had never seen a man die before.

11

The mother clutched her son to her breast, looking away from it all, holding Jason's face toward the stream.

The attractive young woman took off her bonnet and let her long blonde hair billow out. She looked at Cain and nodded.

"You don't have to shoot me. I'm the one person here you can trust, even more than your gang. And I can prove it." As she talked she began unfastening the buttons on her blouse. Quickly she stripped it off, showing the straps of her chemise and the white garment itself that covered her to the waist. She pulled the tail out of her skirt and pulled the chemise over her head. She wore nothing under it.

Her breasts were full and lightly nippled in soft pink. The mounds were rounded and swung slightly outward. She smiled and dropped the chemise and walked toward Cain with a calculated slowness that made her hips grind invitingly.

"I get all the women I want in town," he said.

"Not like me. Give me a chance to show you."

Cain slowly reloaded his .44, this time putting in six bullets. "Why should I?"

"I'm a dance hall girl. A specialist. I do all the things the other girls won't do."

"Anything?" Cain said, his interest caught.

"Anything. Everything." She undid a button at her waist and the skirt dropped into the dust. A moment later she pulled down her petticoats, kicked them to the side of the road and stood naked in the glare of the noonday sun.

"My God, but you are beautiful!" Cain said softly. "Right here, in the middle of the god-damned road!" he shouted.

"Of course," she said and sat down, then lay in the dirt, her legs spread, her knees lifted. "Come on," she invited. "The first one is fast. The second time is always better. Then the third and fourth and fifth I'll make you scream with delight. I told you I'm a specialist."

One of the robbers came up, got off his horse and searched the drummer. He put his hands over the mother and her son to be sure they didn't have weapons. The woman slapped him, and he shrugged, making sure his mask stayed in place.

He strode toward Cain who stood over the girl, rubbing the bulge in his pants near his waist.

"We've got to get out of here!" the second robber said. "We have what we came for."

"Not all of it," Cain spat. "I want her, six different ways."

"We don't have time," the robber said. "We have to figure out what to do with Zack. We can't leave him here dead. What we going to do with Zack?"

Cain slapped him across the face.

"Shut up! Just shut up. One fucking

problem at a time. First this bitch."

He dropped on his knees in the dust between her legs and saw the swollen, red slash through the dusting of reddish crotch hair.

"You got yourself a deal, bitch. Hot and hard and fast. I'll make you cry for more!" Cain tore open his pants and went down between her legs jamming at her, and then with a cry he plunged into her, thrusting forward savagely. There was no feeling, no passion, only the raw edge of lust in his face as he pumped a dozen times and screeched as he climaxed.

In front of the stagecoach, the mother shielded Jason's eyes, but she watched, unable to pull her gaze from the pair writhing in the dust, the woman doing everything to satisfy the man.

The drummer beside her had his hand in his pocket and had turned toward the coach. He was making small sounds in his throat and the woman looked away from him. By the time the duet had played out in the dust, the third horseman came up and talked with the second. They kept the group covered and together put their dead robber friend back on the horse and tied his hands and feet together under its belly. The horse shied and pranced, not used to the strange position of the load, and nervous about the smell of death that clung to the area.

Cain sat back on his haunches, his shrunken penis already put away and his pants buttoned. He reached for his weapon, pushed the muzzle toward the girl's crotch and saw her crawl away in terror.

"Hell, I thought you were supposed to be something special," he said, the cocked six-gun tracking her.

"You promised! The third and fourth time, tonight! It will be fantastic then! No!"

Cain smiled, nodded, then his eyes glazed with ice, his jaw froze in place and a small tic pulsed below his left eye. For just a moment his lower lip quivered, then he shot her in the heart. The dance hall girl flopped backward into the dirt and the mother by the stage screamed.

Cain spun toward the hysterical woman. He was still on his knees.

"Shut up!" he shouted. "I can't stand women who scream that way!"

The woman fell to the ground, screaming again, holding her frightened son trying to protect him. Cain fired four times. All four shots hit the pair and they died without another sound.

The drummer looked at the grisly scene and bolted for the trees. Cain swore, fired once but missed. His pistol was dry. He grabbed his rifle, stood and aimed carefully. His third shot caught the salesman in the back and flung him to the ground, half in and half out of the stream.

"Make sure," Cain told one of the men with him.

"Not a chance," the man said. "You are

plumb crazy in the head. I don't even know you no more."

Cain snorted, walked toward the drummer who was trying to crawl from the stream. He shot him twice in the side of the head and walked back to the stage.

"You got the strongbox?" Cain asked.

"Yes, and it has the double eagles," the second robber said. "We split them here. Fifty each and you get Zack's share. I don't want any of his."

Cain nodded. "Fine. Any other problems?" As he spoke he turned and shot the stage-coach's lead horse in the head with his rifle. It screamed as only a wounded horse can and fell, dragging the other lead horse down. Cain then shot all six horses in the head making sure they were dead. Next he took out a packet of stinker matches and set the stage coach on fire.

The two men who had helped him make the robbery watched from their horses. The smaller of the two spoke.

"We're riding in to town, right down the road. We were in a hunting accident and Zack got shot. An accident, stupid, but he's dead. We thought you should know."

"Where am I going to be?"

"Not with us. You go back to your place or set up an alibi or whatever you want. From now on, I don't know you, never have known you. And don't swing that rifle this way or you are one dead crazy man!"

Cain took a deep breath and nodded. "Yeah, alibi. I'll watch the road and make sure this fire burns good, then I'll fix myself up with a good alibi for all day. Nobody seen us. Should be easy. All day alibi, you two sure as hell better do that too."

They nodded, took the lead line from Zack's mount and moved down the road at a four miles to the hour walk. They would be into High Prairie about three that afternoon.

It took Cain a half hour to feed the fire and make sure that most of the stage burned. He used the girl's blouse and clothes to help it burn, then threw in some pine limbs and pitch sticks. When he left he had a hundred double gold eagles in his saddlebags.

Not bad for a day's work. Two thousand dollars! He turned his roan down the road, then cut cross country heading for his father's Box H ranch. It would take too much time. He was west of town, his father's place was north. Town was closer. That's when he thought of Pauline at the Pink Petticoat Saloon. He could talk her into anything. She would be as good an alibi as he could get for today. If that didn't hold up, it wouldn't matter much anyway. Which meant he would be out on the road. But not yet. He had a lot of choices before that one.

Cain Haworth rode hard for town. It was about five miles, and if he pushed the horse he could go around the three riders in front of him and get there in a half hour or maybe less. The horse wouldn't be much good, but what the hell, it was just a horse.

Cain shoved the rifle deep into the boot, raked his spurs down the roan's sides and jolted down the road at a hard gallop.

# Chapter Two

Cain Haworth stood over the naked girl in the crib above the Pink Petticoat Saloon. She had one small bruise on her left breast, and sobbed as she nodded in agreement.

"Yes, yes! I'll say anything you tell me. I've been sick most of the day and haven't had any customers. I'll say you were here all day. Yes!"

Cain smiled. It helped to know where to hit a girl so she didn't bruise. He caught her breasts and petted them. Kissed them separately and then pushed her down on the bed. She was smaller than the girl from the stagecoach, her tits were tiny, her hips not so wide. He shook his head and stood.

Cain was tall and solid. In these days when the average man's height was five feet nine, Cain was half an inch under six feet. Broad shoulders and a narrow waist gave him a swaggering look as he walked with long strides. The scar stood out whitely now as color tinged his face.

"You just be damn sure you know what to say if I need you to say it. Now I got to go meet some folks coming into town." He ran his hand down her belly and to her crotch and probed for a minute. He laughed softly as she reacted.

"You stay ready, Pauline, good and ready. I'm still all jazzed up and I need about six more today, six different ways. You be thinking up some new positions."

Cain strode out of the room, down through the saloon and waved at Miss Claudine, who owned the saloon, the whores, the gambling hall, the whole shooting match. She had to be worth thousands.

In the street Cain slowed, meandered down Main toward the west looking for the two riders and a body. Then should be along soon. He had passed them two miles out of town.

Cain saw nobody coming down the road, so he leaned against the hardware store wall and rolled a smoke. Bull Durham in a sack. He'd been smoking since he was ten. If he put his mind to it he could roll a smoke with one hand.

The "weed" was half gone when he saw them coming. They rode faster as they hit the outskirts of the little town of High Prairie. It wasn't much of a place. Main Street ended in the road leading east and west. There were three blocks with businesses on both sides, and two blocks of houses behind them. That was the whole thing. The population sign at the west end said the town had 384 people, but that must be when everyone was in town on Saturday night.

Cain watched the little caravan pick up a following. The sheriff's office was in the basement of the courthouse along with the two jail cells. The courthouse stood in the center of town half a block back from the street with a lawn and a small park in front of it.

By the time the two riders and the corpse got to the courthouse there were thirty people, mostly men and kids following them.

The sheriff heard about the body and came out to the street to meet them.

Cain had wandered that way with the crowd and listened as his two friends swung down from their mounts.

"Who is your friend?" Sheriff Quigley asked. Quigley was duly elected in Whitewater county, and had a star to prove it. He was a short man, wearing a black suit and vest and a pure white, high crown hat. He did not wear spurs and rode a horse only when absolutely necessary. He preferred a light buggy.

Jim Darlow cut the body free and eased it to the boardwalk the county had built along the front of the park.

"Sheriff, this here is Zack Kinsey. Friend of mine. We was hunting and he was messing around with his forty-four and he shot himself. Wasn't nothing we could do for him."

The lawman looked at the other rider.

"You know me, Sheriff Quigley. I'm Roger

21

Olsen. That's what happened. We was looking for a buck up along Tinder Creek and Zack was trying to fast draw and dropped his iron and it went off. Shore wish the Doc had been there."

A small man in black suit and a black beard hurried up. He looked at the sheriff who nodded. The undertaker asked a pair of men to carry the corpse to his parlor and the sheriff motioned to the two riders.

"Come inside and we'll fill out some papers. Danged foolish thing to do, shoot yourself that way." He paused. "Didn't you boys get into some trouble a few months back?"

Darlow shrugged. "Nothing serious, Sheriff. Just a little fist fight about a card game. Happens to everybody."

The lawman nodded. "Your weapons been fired?"

"Sure, Sheriff. We been hunting." Darlow said it. "We had a shot at a big buck, but he got away. Then we were plinking at rabbits with our revolvers."

The sheriff said something that Cain couldn't hear and the three went into the sheriff's office. Cain smiled and relaxed his hand that had hung close to his .44. The damn sheriff was just plain stupid. He would believe anything. Almost anything.

Cain walked away as the crowd scattered, the excitement over. He wanted to stay in town for a good tussle with Pauline, but he had a feeling he should get back to the ranch. He might even work a few days just to get on the good side of his father. He never knew when his old man's help might be needed again.

Cain shivered as he thought about how the girl had looked sitting there in the dust of the road just before he shot her. As he pulled the trigger on her he had climaxed. The same thing happened when he shot the woman and the boy and then the drummer. Crazy! Wild! But he was really fucked out. He couldn't do any good with Pauline tonight anyway. He went to the livery and picked up a second horse he kept there to ride the four miles north to his father's ranch.

First thing he would do when he got back to the home place was hide the hundred gold eagles. He wouldn't spend any of them for a while. Gonna be old Billy Hell kicked up about this stage robbery. But they weren't going to find out who did it. Not a chance!

# Chapter Three

Spur McCoy swung down from the stage coach and looked at the little town they called High Prairie. Not much, even by outback Montana standards, but it would have to do. And somewhere around here was a wanton, crazed killer. He had been in Helena on some other business when word came through about the massacre of the stage crew and passengers.

What brought Spur to the case was that this was the fifth robbery of the U.S. Mails on this same stage line within six months. The Postmaster General had screamed to President Grant after the fourth robbery, and Spur had been alerted to watch the situation. Now the Secret Service would spring into action. West of the Mississippi that meant Spur McCoy.

Spur walked across the street to the town's one hotel, the Plainsman, and registered. He got a second floor room with a view of main street.

Spur was a big man at six-two and two hundred pounds of iron hard muscles and bone. His dark brown hair had hints of red and he wore muttonchop sideburns that met his full moustache. Flinty green eyes stared at the world under thick brows. His favorite hat which he tossed on the bed in room 212 was a low crowned brown Stetson with a ring of Mexican silver coins around the band. For the trip he had worn denim pants, a blue shirt and a tan vest.

He unbuckled the wide leather gunbelt and draped it over the brass rail on the foot of the bed. In the leather rested his trusty Colt Peacemaker .45. It had a mother of pearl handle with a screaming eagle engraved on it, as well as more engraving on the barrel, cylinder and housing. He had taken it off an outlaw in New Mexico who no longer had any use for it. He found that the balance and fit suited him fine.

Spur McCoy was one of a small number of federal law enforcement officers who belonged to the United States Secret Service. The service was established by an act of Congress in 1865 with William P. Wood as its first and continuing chief. It began with the purpose of protecting U.S. currency from counterfeiting. Then as other problems came up, there were no other federal law officers, and the Secret Service gradually took on any law problems that could not be or was not being handled by local lawmen.

McCoy joined the service soon after the act was passed in 1865. He served for six months in Washington, D.C. before he was transferred to head the office in St. Louis where he became a force of one handling all problems west of the Mississippi. He found out he was chosen because he had been in the army and had won the service marksmanship contest. He was also the best horseman of the group.

He had just unbuttoned his vest and was wondering how he could arrange for a bath, when there was a knock on his door. Immediately a key unlocked it and a woman backed into the room carrying an armload of fresh linen. Once inside she pushed the door closed with her foot and then turned.

She was a pretty twenty-one, long red hair that flowed almost to her waist. Green eyes that sparked at him in a pert face with high cheekbones and a small nose and delicate chin. She dropped the linen by the door and put her hands on slender hips posing for him. She wore a tight white blouse and floor sweeping brown skirt.

"Mr. McCoy, is your room all right? If not, I'm here to fix it for you." She paused and grinned pointedly. "And to offer any other services which you might desire."

Spur smiled. He had been busy in Helena and had not had the company of a pretty girl for longer than he wanted to remember.

"Do you give baths?" he asked, his ruggedly handsome face breaking into a wide grin.

"Only if I get to have one too," she said.

"Good. How do we start?"

She popped the buttons open on her blouse and walked toward him. She was shorter than he was and reached up on tiptoe and pulled his face down and kissed his lips. Her blouse billowed open and her breasts peeked out. Spur's hand found one and she murmured in response. His hand rubbed the mound and he felt its heat singe his flesh.

"Do you want the bath before or after?" she asked, pulling her lips from his for a moment.

Spur picked her up and carried her to the bed. He put her down, spread her blouse and nuzzled her breasts, then kissed the heavy brown nipples.

"I think I want the bath in between somewhere."

She giggled and slipped the blouse off her shoulders and tossed it to the floor.

Spur moved to the door and braced the room's straight backed wooden chair under the doorknob. He pulled the blind down on the window and went back to the bed. She sat up, her breasts looking much larger now.

He sat down beside her. "What's your name?"

"Vivian. Call me Vi."

"Hi, Vi," he said and kissed her mouth. Spur felt her tremble. He came away. "You've made love before?"

"Oh, yes. I'm older than I look. Sometimes I see a man like you who just makes me melt. I want to run right up and undress in front of him. Is that bad?"

"Of course not. It could be dangerous for you, but not bad. It could get you in trouble."

"I can't get pregnant. I never will. I'm not right inside somehow. My husband threw me out. That was in Denver."

"I'm sorry."

"That was a year ago. I'm used to it now. He wanted six kids. He was a farmer. Needed boys, he said."

She unbuttoned Spur's shirt and ran her fingers through his thick mat of chest hair. "I adore a man with hair on his chest. I don't have any there."

"Good." He bent and kissed her breasts and she wailed, then her hips pumped and she pushed him down on the bed, her slender hips pounding a tattoo on him. Her cry came low and steady, like a call for more, a cry for something not possible. Tears welled out of her eyes, and she sniffled. She brought one of his hands up to her breasts.

In thirty seconds her sudden climax was over and she sat up, wiping the tears from her cheeks.

"My former husband hated that. Sometimes I get worked up and have to let it come out. Does that bother you?"

"No. I enjoy watching a woman have a climax. Do you really work here at the hotel?"

"Sure. That's why I have a pass key, and I get to use a room on the top floor unless we're all full, which ain't happened yet in a year."

Spur's hand moved to her breasts. He petted them and she purred like a kitten.

"Oh, Lord but that feels good! Just about the best feeling there is, I guess, for a woman. That is next to you being inside me, actually fucking." She looked up quickly. "My old man used to hit me whenver I said that word. You mind?"

"No."

She had his shirt unbuttoned and took it off. "This get you excited, my undressing you?"

"I was excited the minute you came into the room."

She smiled. He liked what it did to her face. She shook her shoulders and made her big breasts bounce and roll and jiggle. She watched him as she did it. "You like that?"

Spur bent and kissed both orbs. "There are men who like a girl's legs, and men who dote on a girl's breasts. Me, I'm a tit man."

Vi laughed. "Good. I can help out there. When I was growing up these things embarrassed me. And boys kept pawing at me and touching them. Now I'm glad I got big ones. God, would you kiss them again?"

Spur licked her nipples, then kissed them, and sucked half of one breast into his mouth. She gasped and then sighed and played with the long hair down his neck.

"That is soooooooo good! I love it!" She

pushed him away and stood. "Up here so I can take your pants off. I want to see your good stuff, too."

He stood and felt strange as she undid his belt and then opened his fly. She pulled down his pants and the short underwear he had on. His penis swung out like a big stick and she gasped, then giggled.

"Oh, yes! My goodness, such a big boy! We know just what to do to him to relieve that dangerous swelling!"

She pulled his boots off, then his pants and quickly stepped out of her skirt. She wore a pair of ladies drawers, tight at the waist, with loose legs that came to her knees. They were of white cloth with half a dozen pink ribbons on them. She lay down on the bed and held out her arms.

Vi was shivering.

He lay down beside her and held her in his arms. She rolled over until her body touched his all the way down, then she sighed.

"I still get worried," she said so quietly he could barely hear. "He rejected me so many times. I wanted him and he said it was useless, that I was useless, I should be a whore somewhere. I couldn't have kids so what good was I. Even now, when we're like this, I still worry. I mean . . . I mean . . . I wonder if you're going to laugh at me and send me away too."

"Your former husband wasn't a man. He didn't want a wife, he wanted a little bitch, he wanted a country girl cow who he could breed every year for another free farm hand son. If I ever seen him I'll punch his eyes shut."

She snuggled closer to him. He could feel the heat of her body penetrating his own. She writhed against him and her hand found his erection. He petted her breasts and then kissed her, working his tongue into her mouth.

She sighed.

His hand worked lower to her drawers and slowly he rubbed along her leg, working higher.

"You don't actually have to seduce me, but it is nice," she said. She moved away from him, sat up and wiggled and slid the drawers off her hips and down her legs. She kicked them onto the floor and lifted up on her knees, her legs spread slightly.

"Here I am," she said.

A "V" of dark red hair clothed her crotch. Her hips were as sleek and slender as he had guessed.

"Come down here, I want you," Spur said, a husky wheeze filtering his words.

She yelped in delight and fell on top of him, then rolled over so he was on top.

"Darling, sweet man, please make love to me!"

Spur bent and sucked on each breast, then moved her hand to his erection and his own hand found her crotch.

She began talking, talking fast, not expecting any response. It was a defense mechanism Spur decided.

"I was a virgin when I married. Yes, I had been good, and careful, and lucky. Once one of my uncles came to the house when I was about sixteen and the folks were gone. He kept rubbing himself and started talking bad and told me what he was going to do for me. He would introduce me to the marvels of intercourse. I was frightened to death, but he was older and stronger than I was. He took his penis out of his pants and I almost fainted. I'd never seen one before. I hit him with a pan from the kitchen and ran next door to the neighbors."

Spur touched her crotch and she shivered. He delicately worked around her outer lips and she relaxed a little. Then he rubbed them and she sighed and whimpered in relief and delight.

"Oh, yes, darling. Yes, that's so good!"

He probed with one finger inside her and she screeched and climaxed again. He held his hand over her mouth as she yelled and bounced and humped for a solid minute before she tapered off.

Tears worked down her cheeks as she lifted up to kiss his lips. She lay down and stared at him.

"Oh, lord but you are tender! So thoughtful and loving. Why don't we just get married? Yes, for right now we are married and I don't need to hold back at all. Married! Yes and I can love you, and love you, and . . . fuck you!''

She began a steady stroking of his erection and he stopped her. She smiled.

"Just wondered if he was still loaded."

Spur moved over her and she shook her head. She squirmed out from under him and got on her hands and knees. She pushed her hips up toward him, presenting her red love lips to him. Spur nodded and knelt behind her. The rear entry was quick and easy. She was more than ready.

As he penetrated her she wailed in pleasure. He couldn't get a hand over her mouth now. Half the guests in the hotel would know what was going on in room 212. Spur shrugged. There probably weren't that many registered.

He began moving slowly and she gripped him with hidden muscles on every stroke, and to his surprise was "milking" him. With that kind of encouragement it didn't take long to excite him.

Vi began to build before he did and soon she was shouting and wailing and moaning as if she were on fire. Soon she fell to the bed flat on her stomach and he went with her. The increased tightness drove his own desire to the exploding point and he planted his seed deep within her and then lay gently on top of her.

"You can squish me right into the mattress," she said. "I love the feeling."

They lay there for ten minutes, then he got up and sat on the side of the bed. She sat up beside him, touching his chest with her hand, then stroking the side of his rugged jaw.

"You are simply perfect, Spur McCoy. Do you know that? There is nothing in the whole world like a good man! Nothing. I've known the other kind. When we get our clothes on after a while I will ask you to marry me. Why is it the man's place to do the asking? Not fair. A bath. Were you . . . us . . . we going to have a bath? I think so." She looked at him. Spur nodded.

"Yes, I know so. I better dress a little so I can get some bath water brought up. We do it right in our room here. No separate bathroom, which makes it nicer."

A half hour later Vi had made arrangements and a man brought a round wash tub and three buckets of hot water up to the room. He came back with a bucket of cold water and a big towel and a bar of soap.

"You first," Spur said, and Vi laughed and slid out of her skirt and blouse as he poured in two buckets of hot water and then half a bucket of cold.

Vi stepped in gingerly, then sat down and crossed her legs. She fit in the tub snugly. Spur began washing her and concentrated on her breasts. She laughed.

"Please don't wash them off. I'm going to need those tits to get you back to bed."

Spur laughed. "Sorry. I told you I'm a tit man."

He scrubbed her back, helped her wind her long red hair into a knot on top of her head so it wouldn't get wet. Soon it was his turn and they played for another fifteen minutes, adding the last of the hot water.

Vi washed his genitals carefully, then slowly she began to excite him. Minutes later he stood from the tub, grabbed her and walked her to the bed. They both tumbled on the sheets, wet and soapy and laughing.

They made love again, slowly, with all the tenderness and discovery of a wedding night. At last they lay on the sheets side by side, watching each other, talking softly, becoming more adult and more serious.

"I'm glad I broke in on you today," she said.

"I'm glad too."

"No, I mean because you are a good person. You didn't just use me, you let me participate, you let me enjoy the lovemaking too. I've never really had a chance to do that before."

They were silent a moment.

"You should have. Your husband should have helped."

"I know. Now, I know. I should go. There are a lot of beds to be made."

"Will you get in trouble?"

"No. The owner of the hotel understands. He doesn't bother me. But he expects me to go see him every Saturday night in his rooms."

"Oh. I could have a word with him."

"No. It's practical. I get by. I'll find someone who wants to take care of me. I've been
here less than a year."

"Vi, I hope you find someone. I really do.
You deserve something better than these one
night flings."

Tears crept into her eyes. Vi blinked.
"Thank you." She dressed slowly. Spur
watched. When she was dressed he stroked
her breasts through the material, then kissed
her gently and led her to the door.

"Good bye, nice man," she said.

Spur dressed, checked the time by the
Waterbury watch on a leather thong in his
pocket. Almost due for supper. He dressed in
fresh clothes, another pair of denims, blue
shirt and his soft leather vest, then went
downstairs to the dining room and had
supper as soon as the place opened. He
needed a good meal on his stomach because
he planned to tour the saloons tonight on a
fact finding trip. He wanted to be ready to do
some drinking.

# Chapter Four

Spur McCoy lifted his first lukewarm beer at the Silver Dollar Saloon. He sat at the bar and listened. He heard a little talk about the robbery and the murders, but the story was a week old by then. He stood near the poker and faro tables listening, but again heard nothing to help. Generally saloons were the best spots in town for the local gossip. Not this one.

He went by the sheriff's office and jail, but a deputy said the head man was home. He'd be in the office by eight the next morning unless something happened tonight and he was needed. Spur thanked the young man and hit another bar.

The Naked Lady saloon produced little more than the first one. He did learn that the two biggest ranchers in the area were the Box H and the Lazy L. Both were good sized operations with 20 to 30 hands. The rest of the ranches, about a dozen, were small and usually fighting the larger ones over one thing or another.

A notice tacked on a wall outside the next saloon advertised that the great Tom Ashworth and his traveling thespians would be in town the following month to present the greatest play in the English language, *Hamlet* by the bard himself, William Shakespeare.

The Secret Service man smiled, imagining the reception Hamlet's soliloquy would get from the raw and rought ranchers and townsmen. The actors would be lucky to get out of town alive.

It made him think back. He could have stayed in Washington with the service. That was more the life Spur had been used to. He had been born in New York City and went to Harvard in Boston graduating with the class of 1858. His father was a well known merchant and importer in New York City, and after college, Spur went to work for him. Then the war came and Spur joined the army with a commission as a second lieutenant, and advanced to a captain's rank before Lee surrendered. After two years in the army he was called to Washington, D.C. by Senator Arthur B. Walton, a long time friend of the family. He served as an aide to the senator for almost two years. Perhaps he should have stayed in Washington and the exciting life of high level politics.

He shrugged. He was contented. The life out here in the West was exciting and there was always something different happening. He saw the Last Chance saloon across the street where a drunk was being hustled to the boardwalk and pitched into the dust beside a wagon. Maybe there would be some action there.

Five dance hall girls circulated among the tables, accepting the pats and pinches with little more than a wince and bringing drinks when customers ordered them. All five were tired and no longer young. It seemed to be a slack night.

Spur ordered a beer in a mug and worked on it slowly as he absorbed the local culture. Again he learned almost nothing. It had been a long day, and the bouncing in a stage always left him bruised and exhausted.

Vi hadn't helped his energy level with her ministrations. He left the saloon, by-passed the last drinking and gambling establishment, the Pink Petticoat, and decided he could investigate that one the next day. He would get a good night's sleep and talk to the sheriff bright and early.

When he got back to the hotel room nobody was inside waiting for him. No pretty girl knocked on his door. Nobody shot at him through the window. He put the chair under the door knob again and went to sleep. The bed was a cross between a rock and a lumpy pine log, but at last he slept.

After a quick breakfast of ham and eggs and coffee, Spur went to call on the sheriff. Thurgood Quigley was not Spur's idea of the right kind of a sheriff for a town like this one. He sat in the office as the sheriff finished his breakfast at his desk. Spur had told the sheriff his connections, his authority, and asked the sheriff for total cooperation.

"Most impressive, Mr. McCoy. Your credentials. I've never met a Secret Service man before. Never even knew there were any. About the stage robberies. You said five of them. Quite right. I have it all on file. Mail taken and never found. Some important documents from what various townspeople have said. I trained as a lawyer, did I tell you that?"

"Yes, Sheriff, you did. Do you have any kind of a file on these robberies at all? Any suspects? Have you questioned anyone?"

"No. No clues. That's not my long suit, Mr. McCoy. But you get me a case in court and we'll win it every time!"

Spur looked out the window. "What you're telling me is that you have done nothing about a series of five robberies, the last of which resulted in six murders, including two women and a small boy?"

"Oh, I've asked questions." The small man in the black suit, black tie and black vest shifted in his chair. "It is just that I have no suspects."

"Have any other acts of violence taken place in the past week? Anyone shot, any houses burned down, any vigilante hangings?"

"I should say not! Nothing like that. We're a law abiding town." He paused. "Just that one hunter who shot himself when he dropped his revolver. Ridiculous little episode. Like I say, we're a small cow town trying to keep things pasted together. Times are getting hard. Banks having a tough time. One man I know in Chicago predicts we're going into a depression. He says it could last for five years."

"That's about when we'll solve this case. Do you have time to ride out to the scene of the crime with me?"

"Yes. When?"

"Right now. Let's go."

"Oh, well, I'll have to get my buggy hitched up."

Spur frowned. "You can't ride a horse?"

"Not when I can ride a buggy. Much easier on the back and kidneys. I'll meet you out front of the livery stable in five minutes."

An hour later Spur and the sheriff walked around the scene of the ambush and slaughter. Spur kicked several rifle casings from the dust in the road. Spencer repeating rifle casings. He pocketed them.

The charred remains of the stage had been dragged off the road and down a little slope by a team of horses. Near the same area lay the remains of the six horses. Parts of them had been torn off by predators and vultures. The exposed flesh was putrid and crawling with maggots. The stench was overpowering.

The sheriff left his rig and walked toward the remains.

"This coach has been deliberately burned," Spur said. "Not just torched and left. It's been tended, so more of it would burn. Why, Sheriff?"

"No idea, Mr. McCoy."

"And the horses were all shot in the head with rifle bullets. Why, Sheriff?"

"I don't know. Nor do I know why the robbers killed all six persons on the stage."

Spur nodded thinking out loud. "The shotgun guard and even the driver could have been shot in the ambush. But why the passengers? If the shotgun guard was killed in the first attack, and the driver or one of the passengers identified one of the robbers, that could have been enough."

"Could they have been killed so they couldn't identify the robbers?" the sheriff asked.

"Possibly. It's the only reason I can see. You said one of the women was naked when found?"

"Yes, and the undertaker said she had been sexually attacked, raped."

"Well, now. It seems you know quite a little about this crime, Sheriff. All we need to know is who did it. Who found the bodies?"

"A cowboy coming along the trail looking for work. He came riding in like thunder and banged on my office door."

"The people on the coach related to anyone in the area?"

"The woman and her son. Her husband has

a small ranch out of town to the south along the Santiam. He had a cabin ready for them. They came over from Helena. The man on the stage was a hardware salesman, and we don't know anything about the young woman."

"The widower. Did he have any enemies who might do this?"

"Not possible. He's a quiet man, good natured, thrifty. No enemies as far as I know. It's simply a dead end. I don't know where to start."

"Doesn't look easy. I'll go talk with the widower. Do you have any bad apples in town? Anyone always looking for a fight? Maybe someone who has been losing too much gambling?"

"Not that I've heard about. When a newcomer rides into town it makes big news. We don't have a paper, and people tend to talk. We don't get many drifters. Nothing to come here for."

"So that means the robber and the killers must be people from right here in the community."

The sheriff walked back toward the trail where his buggy sat.

"I hadn't carried it that far, Mr. McCoy."

"Nothing else here I can see, let's get back to town. On the way I want you to tell me everything you know about the two big ranches. I don't see how they could fit in, but they might somehow. What are they, the Box H and Lazy L?"

The lawman told Spur the story of both ranches. The owner of the biggest was Henry Haworth, a large, tough man who came here twenty years ago and founded his empire. He bought land, and gambled for some more, and now the sheriff wasn't sure how much of the land he claimed that he actually owned.

"Haworth is something of a rascal, but he's never been in any real trouble with the law as I remember back near ten or twelve years. He and his wife have three grown sons. Must be 19 or 20 up to about 23. Abel, Cain and Lot. His wife is religious. The boys whoop it up in town now and then but no real problems. I'd say the youngest, Cain, is in town more than the other two.

"Two years ago we had a real dry summer and water got short in the Santiam. There was some talk about damming up the river and since Haworth is the ranch highest on the Santiam, he would get all the water. The ranchers down below talked about organizing and fighting for the water, but then along came three heavy rains about a week apart. and all the springs started running again and the problem was solved.

"I went out and checked out Haworth's place. He showed me the ditch he dug and where he would put some water if he needed to save it. Had a regular sluice gate built and put in so he could open it if he needed to. But that all blew over."

"Looks like it's been a dry summer here,"

Spur said. "Is the same problem coming up again?"

The sheriff frowned. "It might. But I'll have a ruling from the Territorial legislature before then."

"What about the other big rancher?"

"That would be Efrem Longley. Part of his Lazy L ranch is across the river from part of the Box H. Most of the Box H is north and upstream on the Santiam. Efrem is one of the nicest men I know. He's community minded. He's a smart, hard working rancher and a deacon in the town's only church. He's a good neighbor. Efrem and his wife have three daughters, about a year younger than the Haworth boys."

"Is Haworth overgrazing? Docs he graze and control public lands out there?"

"Most big ranchers do. No law against grazing free range."

"But there is a law against controlling it, fencing it, running other people off it. Does Haworth do that?"

The sheriff sighed. "Indeed he does. We've had a complaint or two about homesteaders being run off. No real violence, but enough loud and angry talk so the peaceful kind move on. Haworth pushes the law as much as he can. I'm concerned now about the dry spell. It isn't as bad as it was two years ago, but the time is getting close. It's got to rain in the next two weeks or we're going to have trouble."

"Range war over water?"

"Some would call it that. It means big problems."

"I have enough work finding the killers of those six people."

They rode in silence for a while. The trail followed the Santiam the last half mile into town, and Spur saw that it was well below where the channel seemed to be. There was no "whitewater" now. The water moved slowly, and he could see rocks and water marks on the bank where the level once had been.

Spur couldn't help but ask the question that had been bothering him.

"Sheriff, I was wondering. You don't seem to like the law keeping end of the sheriff's job. Why did you run for the office?"

Sheriff Quigley chuckled. "I ask myself that same question every week or so. I'm a lawyer by trade. I figured it might help me get known if I got elected sheriff. Then after one term I'd open my law practice and be set. Only trouble is there isn't that much work in this little place for a lawyer, and there already was one here. Maybe I'm waiting for old Wilson to die. Then I like the little town, and just decided to say. Been elected four times now. Nothing much ever happens here. Not until now."

"Sheriff, we'll get this one solved and taken care of so High Prairie can go back to a quiet existence. I'll keep you informed of what I do and what I find out. We always work with the local lawmen whenever possible."

Spur could see appreciation in the small man's eyes.

"Thanks, Mr. McCoy, I am pleased you're here. I just don't have the first idea what to do or how to start finding them killers. I'm right proud you're helping."

At the livery, Spur put his rented horse away and hung up the saddle. The livery man had a message for the sheriff.

"Sheriff, Mr. Sullivan, the banker, said you should come and see him just as soon as you got back. He said it was important."

# Chapter Five

Spur listened to the excited message the livery stable man gave to Sheriff Quigley. The lawman looked up at Spur.

"You better come along, McCoy. This banker isn't the kind to get worked up about most anything. It could be important. Seems to me he had a shipment coming in on that stage."

When the two men walked into the bank on the corner of Main and Firist, Marshall Sullivan marched around the high counter the teller used and greeted them with a determined, grim smile.

"Sheriff, I think we have something that reflects on the stage coach robbery." He said it quietly so only the two men could hear. "If you would come into my office." When Spur moved with the sheriff, the banker looked at him sharply. "This is for the sheriff only."

"If it's about the stage robbery, Mr. McCoy here is a part of the investigation," the sheriff said.

The banker nodded and led them into his partitioned off office where they had privacy. He took an envelope from the top locked drawer of his desk and let two double eagles slide out.

"Gentlemen these are brand new 1873 Liberty Head twenty dollar gold pieces. Uncirculated. See how shiny they are, with no nicks or gouges of wear."

Spur looked at them closely. They were uncirculated.

"These coins were due to go into circulation the first of August. All banks and institutions were told to hold the coins until that time."

"You got these on the stage from Denver?" Spur asked.

"We were supposed to get them. Our shipment of two hundred of these coins was on the stage that was robbed, the massacre stage."

The sheriff took another look at the coins. "I hope you know who brought these into the bank, Marshall."

"So far we have it narrowed down to two depositors. Right now we're checking our records to see which one made a deposit yesterday. We should know in a half hour."

"You think these coins came from the stage robbery loot, and that one of the robbers spent them in town," Spur said.

"I know the bankers in Helena. They would not release the coins early. Unless we had a traveler from the east where some banker gave them out early . . ."

"I'd say the chances are good that you have

found our first lead to the robbery, Mr. Sullivan. My congratulations."

As Spur shook the banker's hand, the sheriff introduced them.

"Mr. McCoy is with the United States Secret Service, Marshall. They keep track of our currency among other things."

A clerk came in with a note and Marshall read it and beamed.

"We did have a deposit yesterday. We're ninety-five percent certain that these two double eagles came from the Pink Petticoat saloon deposit."

Spur looked at the sheriff.

"Far as I know the saloon is owned and run by a woman. She's honest and fair. Never much trouble in her place. She has the best bouncer in town, and he keeps the place straight. From what I hear of her I'd say she had no part of the robbery."

"A customer then," Spur said. "Not a lot of men would spend forty dollars in a saloon. That's two months' wages for most of them. Somebody there might remember a big spender."

"Let's take a walk, Mr. McCoy. I'm beginning to enjoy this kind of investigation work. Marshall, I'll take these coins as evidence, but you'll get them back."

They went across the street and down half a block. It was the only saloon in town Spur hadn't checked out the previous night. It was open but almost deserted. The time was a little before noon.

Through the swinging batwing doors, Spur saw the usual western saloon: long bar with a brass rail on one side. The rest of the first floor was taken up with small tables with four chairs around each and a deck of cards waiting. There were three faro tables, and one for throwing dice. Nobody was gambling. One man sat at the bar.

Toward the back was an open staircase that led sharply up to the second floor. Spur guesed the girls would be up there catching up on their sleep before the day's trade began coming in again about five that afternoon.

The barkeep looked up and nodded when he recognized the sheriff.

"Morning, Sheriff, haven't seen you in here for quite some time."

"This is official, Barry. The lady around?"

"In back, I'll tell her you're here. She don't like surprises. Got a minute?"

The sheriff nodded and they sat down at one of the poker tables. Spur picked up the cards and began dealing. He figured it would take any lady ten minutes to get presentable.

It took her twenty. They had played ten hands of seven card showdown poker, and the sheriff won seven of them.

"You should take up gambling," Spur said.

"My luck vanishes when there's money on the table," the small man said smiling.

She came around the end of the bar with a firm step in a business-like dress that any of the matrons in town might wear, tight around the throat, full over the bodice and

51

long sleeves. The lady was about thirty-five and still had a good figure. She was taller than Spur expected, maybe five-seven, and her black hair fell loosely around her shoulders.

Spur stood at once frowning, then he looked closer and began to smile. She was watching the sheriff as she came up and had given Spur only the briefest of glances.

"You always did say you wanted to own your own gambling saloon," Spur said as she stopped in front of them. She looked at him, her polite smile changing to a big grin.

"Spur McCoy! Where in hell did you come from?"

She took two steps and was in his arms, planting a big kiss on his cheek. He hugged her tightly, then let go and she stepped back.

"Spur, it must have been four years. Arizona. Oh, do I remember that last shoot-out! I still say you were lucky that I was along with my .44."

"I was lucky all right." He turned to the sheriff. "I knew this lady before," he said.

"I figured that," the sheriff said with a smile. "Miss Claudine, if you would sit down, I have some official business. Hate to interrupt a reunion, but duty calls."

"Yes, of course." She held Spur's hand as he led her to the chair and sheriff positioned for her. The men sat down and the sheriff took the envelope from his pocket. There was no one else in the saloon who could hear what they said.

"These two coins were deposited in the bank by your business. Oh, they are genuine, too genuine." He explained to her about the release date of the coins, and the possibility that they were stolen from the massacre stage coach.

"My god! You mean one of my customers might be the killer? The same one who shot those two women and that little boy?"

"It certainly looks that way, Claudine," Spur said. "As you might have figured out, I'm here to find the killers, and get the mail circulating again."

She was resilient, nodding slowly. "Yes, I understand. We do have a big poker game from time to time. Forty dollars. One of the girls might know, or Barry. Let me ask him."

"We need to keep this absolutely secret," Spur said. She nodded and came back a minute later.

"Barry says he can't remember any one person giving him two double eagles over the past two or three days. But he'll watch for those 1873 issue coins from now on. Right now he figures it could be any one of about thirty men."

The sheriff stood. "I need to get back to the office. We will work together on this robbery, won't we, Mr. McCoy?"

"Yes, absolutely."

"Fine." He waved his hat at Claudine, nodded to Spur and walked out the front door.

Claudine caught Spur's hand and they both

stood at the same time.

"I think it's time we had a small celebration. Reunions between old friends like this don't happen very often." She led him toward the back, down a hall and to a door marked PRIVATE. She took a key from a hidden pocket, opened the door and locked it as soon as they stepped inside.

The room was plush looking, like the inside of one of those luxury hotel rooms in New York. A thick rug covered the floor. The walls were decorated with pictures and drapes of expensive silk cloth. An overstuffed sofa sat to one side and a matching chair beside it. Both had been covered in an expensive silk material with fancy embroidery.

To one side sat a stylish writing desk that was open and a file folder and several envelopes near by.

In the center of the room hung a chandelier, one of the old cut glass types with holders for thirty candles.

She paused for a moment to allow him to examine the room, then pulled him forward.

"Wait until you see my bedroom. It is really something."

It was. For a moment Spur thought he had been magically transported into the Arabian Knights. The room looked like the inside of a sultan's tent. A four poster bed huddled at one side of the fifteen-foot square room. The bed was draped with silks and satins. The top of the bed over the four posts was a delicate combination of embroidered silks and swatches of fancy silk, loosely folded and braided into an intricate pattern.

A rug twice as thick as that in the living room spread from wall to wall. The floor was strewn with big harem pillows, and the walls were all covered in fabric, loose and swaying. The scent of incense burned filling the air. He noticed that there were six lamps situated around the room to provide light. That's when he realized the room did not have a window. Light came through a skylight that had been covered with glass. It gave the room a soft, filtered look that enhanced the atmosphere.

"Wow!" Spur said.

"Thanks, that was the nicest thing you could have said. Now do I get a real kiss?"

She flowed into his arms and Spur let the heat of her body's desire pour into him. It triggered memories of Arizona and the frantic, fantastic week they had spent together. As they kissed he picked her up and sat down on the bed.

"Now I think you're starting to get the idea," she said, her eyes still closed, her lips nibbling at his lips, then clamping firmly on his mouth again.

His hands found her breasts and he remembered the upthrust beauties in the buff, marvelously formed, sensitive to his touch. He caressed them and she moaned in delight, then she pulled away from him and spun around.

"Yes, my darling, wonderful Spur. But first I feed you. I remember how much stronger you are after a good meal. Will a half raw steak and a quart of beer suit you?"

He nodded and watched as she unbuttoned the dress and pulled it over her head. Under it she wore a pink chemise that came to her waist, with delicate straps over her shoulders, and her thrusting breasts unrestrained under it. Her petticoats were pink, and he could see at least three of them.

That was when he remembered that she loved to cook almost as much as to make love. And she was an expert at both.

She peeled off one of the petticoats to reveal another one beneath it. "Come on, big guy, let's go into my kitchen and get the steaks started. If you see anything you like, you can chew on it a little as an appetizer."

Her kitchen was eight feet square with a large kitchen range at one side fitted with a hot water coil and reservoir. At the other side she had an ice box that held a chunk of ice they must have cut during the winter and held over in an ice house with lots of straw. The ice bow kept food cool and cold without spoiling.

Claudine took an inch-thick steak ten inches across and put it in a frying pan. Then she stoked the fire and let the meat start to brown in the pan.

Spur reached around her from the back

and clamped one hand over a bare breast. He felt the warmth of the mound.

"Now here is what I like," he said. She twisted in his arms and kissed him, thrusting her tongue deep into his mouth as she did and then retreating. He lifted the chemise off over her head and her breasts swung out as if eager for action.

"Tits!" he said in awe. "Claudine, you have the best set of tits in the whole world!" He took one in his mouth, his tongue fighting with her nipple and Claudine groaned and sagged against him. Then she turned and with a free hand flipped the steak to the other side in the skillet.

"Brown on the outside, red and raw inside. Isn't that the way my man likes his meat?"

Spur laughed. "Steaks that way, but my woman I like as naked as the day she lost her virginity."

Claudine squealed in mock terror and stepped out of another petticoat. She danced away from him and quickly set a small table by a heavily curtained window. Then she came back with a slow wiggle with her hips that left Spur panting.

"Christ, what a decision, do I eat you first or thc stcak first?"

She danced toward him quickly, holding up one breast for his mouth. He bent and accepted it and she pushed against him again, her hand sneaking to his crotch and finding the hardness inside his pants. She rubbed it a dozen times, then pulled away and checked the steak. She moved the skillet back off the hottest part of the stove and put a lid on it.

"You have two minutes," she said.

"Plenty of time," Spur said. He jerked down the last petticoat and then her silk drawers. She stood naked in front of him, one foot at right angle to the other, her chest high and thrust forward, the glistening fur over her crotch dark black like her hair.

"If you see anything you like . . ."

He grabbed her and pushed her against the wall, spreading her legs with a sweep of one hand.

"Right here?" she asked surprised.

He nodded, his fuse burning shorter.

"Anytime you're ready, I'm ready, big lover!" she said. "The gate is wide open, come on inside."

He ripped open his fly and pulled out his shaft.

"Oh, my!" she said. "I had forgotten what a telegraph pole you keep in those britches. "Come on!"

He bent, positioned and thrust. He tried again and then she moved slightly and moaned as he slid into her, his sword into her scabbard as if they had never been apart.

"What do we do now?" she asked and laughed softly. It was an old joke between them.

He showed her. The unnatural position

compensated a little for his full head of steam. But still she began building before he did. When he sensed her almost over the edge he stopped his thrusting, and let her cool off. Then he punched upward again and again, until she was panting and almost ready. He stopped again, pushing fully into her hot enclosure, waiting for her to recover.

The third time she would not be denied. She surged past him and grunted and groaned as she tried to thrust down against him and at last the tremors drove through her again and again until she was spent and ruined for a time.

Her climax triggered his own pent-up desire and he plowed hard into her, lifting her frame off the floor and bringing her to a new rush of emotional release.

Spur thrust again and exploded into her, their pelvic bones grating against each other as he pressed her hard against the wall as his body gave the final spasms of desire.

Her arms came around him quickly.

"If you move for five minutes I'll kill you!" she said.

Both were panting now, with air gushing from them into the air. They heard the steak spitting and sizzling in the iron skillet, but neither could move to take it off the fire.

At last her arms loosened, and he bent his knees coming away from her. She walked to the bedroom and he moved the steak off the fire.

She was back in a minute, still naked, wearing the biggest smile he had seen in months.

"Sir, your woman and your steak are both ready."

Spur laughed softly. It was Arizona all over again. "I think I'll try the steak this time. But it couldn't be half as good as my woman."

# Chapter Six

Spur McCoy put down his knife with his right hand and speared the choice bit of tender, blood red steak with the fork in his left hand and put it in his mouth. For just a moment he closed his eyes as his tastebuds luxuriated in the delicate flavor of the juices from the succulent meat.

"Chef Rene in New York's Savoy hotel could not have cooked it better," Spur said looking up at the deep brown eyes that watched him eating. Claudine was still naked, her breasts resting on top of the small table where she sat relishing every moment of his feast.

Her face showed three pleased expressions, then dancing eyes steadied. "As good as your woman?"

"Almost as good," he said. Spur reached over and kissed her and opened his mouth to share the bit of steak. She sucked some of it into her mouth and smiled as she chewed. There was only one man she would do that with. It was the most personal of all intimacies.

She nodded. "Almost as good."

They both laughed. He stood, as naked as she was. She moved beside him, her arms wrapped around his back her breasts pressing hard into his chest, her crotch pushing against his upper legs.

"Come. Remember in Arizona we ran out of new positions. Have you ever tried 'splitting the reed?' "

Spur shook his head.

"It's kind of wild. I'm on my back with one leg straight up in the air and you kind of upright with my leg on your shoulder and my other leg down flat."

"Show me," he said.

"I was really hoping you would say that."

They made soft sweet love three more times that afternoon, and Spur got to the printer in time to talk him into making up forty hand bills before he quit for the day. The posters were the usual size, twelve by twenty. They all said:

### Federal Law Officer

Now in High Prairie to gather evidence for prosecution of killers of 6 persons on stage coach a week ago. Have definite proof on two killers, need more. Anyone spotting anyone riding into town July 15, contact me at Plainsman Hotel today from 1 to 5 P.M. Room 212. Full protection to all who testify.

He took the handbills and with a box of

thumb tacks posted them on forty of the most favorable walls and posts in town. It was just before dark when he got the last one put up. Already there was a lot of talk in town about the posters. He stopped in two of the saloons and heard all kinds of wild stories. No reward had been offered but he heard several men say they would testify anyway. Nobody should shoot down two women that way, especially the pretty one.

Spur nodded with the majority and went to his room up the back stairs. There was no one outside his door, but he expected company soon. He got into his room, jammed the chair under the door and then made a dummy and put it in his bed so in the darkness it appeared that a man was sleeping. He left the lamp burning on low wick and settled down on a blanket to one side of the window that opened onto a porch over Main Street.

He drifted off at once, but snapped awake. His Waterbury showed that it was slightly after midnight. He nodded again but came awake when the window near him slid up quietly. Spur picked up his already cocked .45 Eagle Butt Peacemaker and waited. A moment later hands appeared, then a head and shoulders as someone came through the window.

The intruder squirmed into the room over the sill, landing on his hands on the floor two feet below the opening. He brought in his feet and stared at the bed. As silently as death his hand brought up a six-inch knife and he held it like a sabre. Clearly the man had used a knife before. He checked the door, then moved on silent feet toward the bed.

He thrust the first time with all the power of his body behind it, striking what he thought was a broad back. The knife went in and he pulled it out and jabbed it twice more into the dummy on the bed. Spur shot him in the right leg and kicked the knife from his hand.

When the booming roar of the .45 faded in the room, Spur could hear the killer wailing.

"Help me! I'm bleeding to death. Stop the blood!"

Spur turned up the lamp, couldn't remember seeing the man around town, and shook his head.

"You tell me who hired you to kill me, and I'll stop the blood. Otherwise, you die right there on the floor in about five minutes."

"Oh, Christ! Don't do that. I can't tell. He said he'd kill me. Oh, Christ, no!"

The would-be killer was a head shorter than Spur, unshaven, dirty, wearing torn range pants and a tattered blue shirt.

"How much did he pay you?" Spur asked.

"Forty dollars. Then forty more when they find you dead in the morning."

"Double Eagles?"

"Yeah."

"Give them to me."

The man swore and handed them over. In

the light Spur could read the date: 1873.

"Eight dollars to kill a man? I must not be very tough."

"Stop the blood!

"Who set me up!"

"I don't know. It was dark, in back of the livery. Guy said to do it and come right back tonight and he would give me the other forty tonight and I could ride out of town."

"If you had gone back there he would have killed you," Spur said.

It was a chance, but all he had. He bent and tied the man's hands behind his neck, put a bandage on the leg wound, stopping the flow of blood. Then Spur tied the ambusher's feet together and cinched up his ankles to his hands, pulling them up tight behind his back.

"Stay there," Spur said. He took the man's hat and his knife and went out the hotel room into the hall. Only one man was there looking down the hall.

"Gun went off when I was cleaning the damn thing," Spur said. The man grunted in sympathy and went back to bed.

It took Spur ten minutes to move from shadow to shadow to the back of the livery stable. There was a chance this second man was also hired, but it was a risk he had to take.

He went into the blackness behind the livery and just this side of the big corral. Nothing. He paused and waited, every one of his thousands of pores and nerve endings reaching for some kind of signal. Nothing.

He moved to the far side of the darkness and crouched, waiting, with his pistol cocked and ready and six rounds in the chamber.

Twenty minutes later he saw movement at the side of the livery. Someone staggered around the corner into the blackness waving a bottle. Then came the sound of breaking glass and the man swore. He sang a dirty little song and then fell against the wall.

Two minutes later a voice sober and cautious whispered.

"Are you there?"

"Yeah," Spur whispered. "I done it."

"Good, come on over here."

Spur could almost see the man snaking the gun out of his belt.

"You come over here," Spur said and rolled silently six feet away from the barn.

The twin flashes of gunpowder around the cylinder and out the muzzle of a six-gun showered the darkness with small streaks of light that were gone almost before the eye could record them.

Spur was ready with his iron up. He tracked in one the flashes, shooting just below them and slightly to the right, giving allowances for a right-hander. He fired twice. The sound of a bullet hitting flesh was unlike any Spur had ever heard, something between a thonk on a watermelon and the sound of the same round hitting water. Both rounds struck home.

"Oh my god! I'm dying!" The man screamed, then he fell.

Spur waited almost five minutes before he moved. No one had come to investigate the shots or the screams. The other man had not moved. Spur went across the open ten yards in a rush and found the body where he thought it would be. There were two rounds near the heart. The man was sprawled backward on his side. Spur found two more double eagles in his pocket. He took them for checking later, but he was sure they would be 1873 double eagles. Wearily he went to find a deputy and show him where the body was.

The deputy on duty nodded as he looked at the man.

"Gus Talmage, a rummy who does odd jobs. He's never rated high enough to be a bushwhacker before. He must have been moving up in the world."

"This is as far as he goes," Spur said. "Tomorrow he goes down, six feet down."

Spur filled out a sudden death statement and said he would check with the sheriff in the morning. As he sat there he flipped two double eagles in the air and caught them. Both were 1873, uncirculated. Now the killer had spent six of them.

Back at Spur's hotel room the deputy took charge of the attempted murder suspect and called Doc Varner out of bed to patch up his thigh. The sawbones was unhappy at the wake-up call and did not treat the prisoner with tenderness.

"Next time you try to kill somebody, young feller, you do a better job of it, then you won't get shot and I won't have to come dig out the damned bullet."

Before Doc was done probing the drunk had stopped screaming, but only because he had passed out.

It was after two in the morning when Spur went back to the hotel, hired another room under a phony name and slept until eight in the morning.

His mouth felt like somebody had slept in it. He had three cups of coffee, a breakfast steak and hashbrown potatoes and an apple, and still he was hungry. Missing sleep always made him hungry. At least his wanted poster had stirred up some comment. He didn't expect much more from it. The real killer had struck and shown his hand. But Spur knew he should be back to check out the locals this afternoon, just in case. That would leave him time to make the ride out of the widower's place and to the Lazy L ranch on the way back. Time, that is, unless he ran into unexpected problems. The sheriff would want to talk about the dead man last night as well as the wounded man Spur dumped in his office after Doc Varner had finished with him.

# Chapter Seven

Spur picked up directions to the widower's ranch at the sheriff's office. It was a six mile ride south of town, and close to the banks of the Santiam, the life blood of this region. The man's name was Ivan Johnson, he was forty-two years old and the sheriff said he was devastated by the loss of his family. He had left them in Helena so they would be safe and have it easier during the winter until he could get a proper house raised for them.

It was one of those visits Spur knew he had to make. From what everyone said it would be totally non-productive, but it was his job, and he was going to do it. The ride out to the ranch was pleasant. The sun played tag with a few high scattered clouds but none of them spelled rain. Spur could see how the size of the little river did not grow as he moved downstream. It barely held its own, and in places looked to be on the verge of drying up. Then new springs would bring it back to life.

The drought was worse than he had thought.

No one answered Spur's knock on the Johnson place door just before ten o'clock that morning. He went out to the barn and found no one. He saw a few cattle in a pasture another mile south and rode down.

A man in overalls and a railroad cap sat on the bank of the stream throwing rocks in the water.

"Sir, could you help me find Ivan Johnson?"

"Me," he said without looking up.

Spur got down from his horse and introduced himself. The man looked older than forty-two. He was gaunt, unshaven but not with a beard. His eyes were red and his hair was tangled under an old hat.

"Mr. Johnson. It's my job to help find the men who killed your family and robbed the stage. I'm going to find them before I leave the county. Do you know of anything that might help me?"

Johnson shook his head, then threw a stone in the water.

"Was someone trying to hurt you by attacking your family?"

"No. Nobody cares that much about us. We're new here."

Spur pressed on, asking the questions he had to, and in the end came up with exactly nothing to help the case. He thanked the man for his help, mounted up and rode north again. He had seen a sign pointing to the Lazy L ranch, just out of town, but noticed that it pointed north of the village instead of south. So he would have to retrace his steps to find the Longley clan. This was not going to be his best day.

Spur pushed the roan and came into the Lazy L about 12:30. With any luck they would not have finished dinner yet and invite him to take a plate. He was surprised to hear the dinner bell ring as he came into the ranch yard.

It was impressive, with three barns, several outbuildings, and a big ranchhouse, a separate cookshack and dining hall for the hands. Two bunkhouses flanked the dining hall.

A hand rode to meet him as he entered the building area.

"Howdy. You're that detective guy I heard about in town," the hand said. "Reckon you want to talk to the boss man. Tie up over yonder and I'll take you up to the big house."

Spur tied his horse and went up to the house. He had put on his formal range wear, a pair of brown pants, a brown lightweight jacket, white shirt and string tie. Now he was glad he had.

Someone stood behind the screen, at the back door waiting. The man was about five-ten, with silver-gray hair that had been black, and a still black moustache and goatee. His eyes crinkled as he smiled and held out his hand.

"I'm Efrem Longley, you must be that detective guy."

Spur took the offered hand, felt the

71

hardness of the skin and healed blisters, and smiled.

"Yes, sir, Mr. Longley. I'm Spur McCoy. Could I have a word or two with you?"

"Dinner time, young man. Us Longley's don't talk much when we eat. Welcome to sit down to the table with us. Be a treat for everybody. Come right in. You can use the vestibule there to wash the dust off your hands, you want to."

Spur said he would and found a table with a bucket of water and a crockery wash basin, dipper, mirror and a line-up of six towels. He washed his hands, combed his moustache and hair and dried on the first towel. Outside the open door he saw a flash of skirt and then it was gone.

Longley met him at the door.

"Right this way and I'll introduce you."

Spur was not ready for what he saw. In the kitchen around the big varnished plank table were four pretty women. One of them had to be the mother, but he was hard pressed for a moment to pick her out. Longley rescued him by introducing her and then naming his daughters.

"The first filly there on the left is Delilah. She's eighteen, and a mite shy. Next is Mary, who is nineteen and wants to be a schoolmarm or some such. My eldest is Bathsheba who we all call Bee, and she can ride and rope better than I can." The girls were all pretty, but Delilah was going to be the beauty.

72

Mary was a little aloof and cool, and Bee had a glint in her eye he had seen before. His place was between Bee and Delilah and Mary was just as happy.

"We're having a party next month, Mr. McCoy, a coming out party for the girls, just like they have back east. I'm inviting all the girls eighteen to twenty-one in the county to be my guests and we'll have an all night dance and announce to the whole country that these lovelies are now ready for marriage."

"Daddy, that's not what it's supposed to be," Mary said. "In New York they have the coming out party to introduce the young ladies to formal society."

"Society, hell. We don't have one here, just the business of getting my daughters married off proper. I told you, the one who claims the best son-in-law will be the one to take over the Lazy L spread."

Mrs. Longley nodded to Spur, and he had a feeling she was used to being left out of things, and that she didn't mind one whit.

Spur soon got the conversation shifted to the weather and the dry land. They ate enough food for an evening meal, roast chicken, corn on the cob, fresh peas and potatoes, and even some early tomatoes and big slabs of fresh baked bread and currant jelly. And pots of coffee.

"What happens if the river dries up, Mr. Longley?" Spur asked.

"If the river goes, I lose all my cattle. Them critters got to drink. Each one needs twenty gallons of water a day. That's a lot of water for five or six thousand head. Course, they all ain't right here. But if the river dries up, the only reason will be because that criminal upstream, Haworth, has shut it off. You heard about the sluice gate he's got? He could change the course of the river anytime he wants to, make it all flow over his land, and I couldn't get a drop of water."

"Mr. Longley, I don't think he would do that. There are laws about rivers. Under normal conditions the upper owner on the river may not deprive the lower owner his fair share of the water for drinking by man and his animals. Each owner along the length of the river is guaranteed enough water for his cattle."

"What happens if it does dry up?"

"That would be called an act of God, and every owner would suffer his losses. But one man can't take all the water and leave the downstream ranchers with none."

"Damn right, I been telling that no good Haworth that for two years. He says what he's got, is his."

"Now, Mr. Longley, you know that this means you have to respect the rights of the ranchers below you. Even if you have to let some of your stock die from thirst, you have to allow enough water through so each rancher below can save the same percentage of his herd that you are saving."

"This is going to get damn difficult. But if there's trouble it will be that damn Haworth. We had a run-in the first day I homesteaded here, and we been clawing at each other ever since."

Longley finished his meal and leaned back. "Glad we got that settled. Now, about the important matters. Which of my darling daughters do you cotton to? All of them are available. Why not pick out one right now before the rush of courting starts?"

"Father, really!" Mary said.

Bee, the oldest, winked at Spur and her father roared. "That's Bee, she'd be a handful for any man. By jingles, I know what we can do! Why don't you have a little courting session with each of my girls right now? Fifteen, twenty minutes in the parlor. Even close the door! See which one you like the best. Sure, I know, you're busy. But you brought such good news about the law and the water, I want to make it up to you."

Spur laughed at the discomfort Mary showed. "We could make it a kind of training. Your girls could practice on me, knowing it doesn't count. How would that be, Mr. Longley?"

"Hell, yes! Mother, you get the cold apple cider and put it out in the parlor, and some of those little cakes. We'll go in order—Bee first before she pops her britches!"

Spur thought Mary was going to bolt out of the room, but she sat and waited her turn. Bee was up and waiting for him. She linked her arm though his and walked him into the parlor.

The heavily varnished door shut with a loud click behind them and Spur had a sense that the parlor was kept closed off most of the time, and used only for special occasions. It smelled a little musty and cool. Bee was neither. She led him to a small love seat with room for two that faced the side wall. The back was to the only door and he helped her sit down, then sat beside her.

At once she leaned in and kissed him, a hot, demanding kiss that soon led to her tongue darting into his mouth. She came away smiling.

"Does that surprise you?"

"A little."

"Papa thinks I'm still a virgin," she said softly and caught one of his hands and put it over her breasts. "Pet them," she said. "Pet them or I'll scream and get you in trouble."

His hand moved over her breasts.

"No, inside!" she said, unbuttoning two of the fasteners.

Her hand slid in with his and pulled aside a garment and his hand closed around her left breast.

Bathsheba sucked in a long breath and shivered in a small climax that froze her face in glory for a moment. Her hands touched his crotch.

"You don't mind if I feel around, do you?" she said and before he could answer she had

76

opened his fly buttons and her hand wormed through his underwear to his stiff manhood.

"Oh, yes, he's so ready! I wish we could do it right here! Right now!"

"No! I don't want to get shot."

She nodded. "Daddy might." She pressed his hand against her breasts again as she wiggled and a tremor swept through her. Then she took his hand out of her blouse, fastened the buttons and pushed his hand under her skirt. "I almost never wear drawers. See!"

His hand found her soft, bare inner thigh and she pushed it higher. "I have an idea," she said. "Do you have a long finger?" He nodded.

"Go ahead, poke me with that!" Then she worked at his crotch and soon had his penis out and standing tall. "If you hear the door jiggle or the latch turn, you pull me up, all right?"

Spur looked at her in surprise, then she bent down and took his erection in her mouth.

"Now I'll really be shot!" Spur said, trying to lift her up. She wouldn't budge, but kept working her mouth up and down on his manhood. She pushed his hand farther under her skirt and Spur found the wetness and drove his finger into her a dozen times, then came out, lifted her away from his throbbing, purple erection and pushed it roughly back into his pants. He buttoned up his fly just before the door rattled, and Mr. Longley strode into the room.

They both looked at him over the back of the padded loveseat.

"Well, I hope you two got to know each other a little. Time is up. Mary is next."

"Good luck, she won't even touch you," Bee whispered. "Just talk, but watch out for little sister, she's getting hot panties again."

Bathsheba stood. Spur stood. He took her hand, thanked her for the enjoyable talk, and she walked out past her father.

Spur felt a touch of sweat on his forehead, and realized how close he had come to filling a newly dug grave.

Mary whispered with her father for a moment, then came in with a scowl.

Spur let her sit down and he stood.

"Mary, I realize this is awkward for you. Why don't you tell me what you want to do with your life? Your father mentioned teaching school. Would you like that?"

She brightened. "Oh, yes! Of course I would need a year of normal school over at Helena, but then I'd be fully qualified. We haven't had a qualified teacher at High Prairie ever. I want to help this country grow, and the best way is to educate our people. I've got lots of books and I read all the time."

Spur let her talk for five minutes, then he sat down beside her. "When I talk with your father, I'll suggest that he send you to normal school. Every town needs a good teacher."

"Oh, would you? I would be ever so grateful." She surged toward him, kissed his cheek and half fell against him pushing her breasts on his chest, then realizing what she had done, she eased back a little. She stayed close to him. "Mr. McCoy, you may kiss me if you wish." She turned her lips to him and he kissed her gently, then moved her away from him.

She still had her eyes closed.

"Mary . . . Mary," he called softly.

Her eyes popped open. "Oh my, that felt so nice! You are the first man I've ever kissed. I did like it. Now I see what Bathsheba is always talking about." She blinked. "But you said you would talk to Father about my going to school. I would be ever so grateful."

Soon the knob rattled and Mr. Longley came in with his youngest, the beauty, Delilah. The girls were all dressed much the same, in modest, but tightly fitting print dresses with long sleeves and high buttoned necks. And they all were clean, sweet smelling and big busted girls. Delilah sat down beside him and smiled.

"Would you like to kiss me?" she said softly.

"No," he said.

She scowled. "Lots of boys want to kiss me. I told them to ask Papa." She turned back smiling. "But you can kiss me if you want to."

Spur leaned in toward her but she leaned away.

"But not until after we talk. Are you staying here long? Have you ever been married? Where did you go to school? How did you turn out to be so handsome?"

He laughed softly at her. "You're scared to pieces, aren't you, Delilah? You don't know what might happen if I kiss you. So just relax. Mary wants to be a teacher. What do you want to do?"

"Get married, I guess. That's what most girls do. Get married and have babies and get fat and get old and die. It does all seem a little pointless, doesn't it?"

"Depends. A lot of wonderful, beautiful, amusing, exciting things can happen almost every day of your life, if you let them happen, if you look for them, watch for opportunities. Like right now. Have you ever been kissed?"

"No. Mama says I should wait and let the boy I'm going to marry kiss me."

"But wouldn't it be exciting, right now?"

Her eyes widened. "Right here? With Papa right out there listening?"

"Kisses are usually rather quiet."

"I don't know."

"Think about it. Now close your eyes." The second she closed her eyes, Spur leaned in and kissed her lips gently, just a brush and moved back.

She opened her eyes. "Was that a kiss?"

"One kind of a kiss."

"Oh! There are different kinds?"

"Yes. Keep your eyes open." He leaned in again and kissed her lips harder this time, and put his arm around her and pulled her tightly against his chest until he could feel her breasts flatten as he held her close. Then slowly he let go of her and eased away from her lips.

"That was a more serious kind of kiss."

"Oh!" Her face was blank. Then she smiled. "I really liked the last one. Could we do that agin?"

The door rattled and opened and they swayed apart as her father came into the room. Spur saw that Delilah was a little flushed, but she stood easily, nodded to her father and walked out of the room.

"Well, well. My little ladies all seemed impressed with you, Mr. McCoy. Remember, you can come courting any of them, at any time."

Spur made his thanks and thanked Mrs. Longley for the dinner and then walked out to the hitching rack with the rancher.

"You go see old Haworth. Tell him about my legal right to water for my stock, and make sure he understands. That way maybe we won't have any trouble. You seen how that water level has been dropping. We need some rain, and damn soon."

Spur told the rancher he would go visit with the other big rancher just as soon as he figured out the murders.

Then he paused. "I hope you consider letting Mary go to Helena to go to normal school. She says the only thing she wants to do is be a teacher. It's an honorable and much needed profession. Consider it." They shook hands and Spur rode back to town. It had been quite a noon time. His watch showed that it was only a little past 1:30. He would have time to talk to some of the people in his room who answered his broadsides . . . if anyone did. Somebody would respond, even if it was a person with no help for him. He rode faster.

# Chapter Eight

Two men and a woman waited outside his room when Spur walked down the hall at the Plainsman Hotel. None of them looked dangerous.

"Are you folks here about the stage coach massacre?"

They all nodded.

"Are you together?"

"No," the woman said.

Spur unlocked the door and invited her inside. He left the door open. She looked at it to make sure it stayed open, then sat down in the chair he provided her.

Five minutes later he was sure she knew nothing about the robbery. He thanked her and she left, smiling.

The first man had seen three men riding into town. One of them was draped over his saddle.

"Was that the hunting accident?"

"What he claimed. Knew that boy. Never did like to hunt. I don't think he was hunting at all. Them ones he was with is kind of nocounts themselves. I'd damn sure check out the three of them. Three could rob a stage."

"But then ride into town with a dead man? That doesn't sound logical." Spur watched the informant closely.

"Hell, yes it does." the man said. He was about forty. Spur had seen him in one of the taverns. "Had me a sheriff's job once down Texas way. Learned what some of these outlaws do, how they think. See, if they come right into town, and claim they got shot hunting, nobody would think a thing. Got to cover up the man getting gut shot and killed somehow. Makes sense."

Spur nodded. "Damned if it don't. What is your name?"

"Udell. Ty Udell. I ain't had work in a spell."

Spur nodded. "Maybe you could work for me for a bit."

"Detective work? Damn sure!"

"Stand over there by the window while I talk to this next man. Keep a watch out to the street and see if anybody is interested in this room."

"Yes sir!"

The last man in the line was drunk. He apparently had been that way for some time.

"Sure, I had a drink, but I know what I saw. Day of the massacre, I saw me one kid come hightailing it into town. He damn near killed his horse. It was all lathered up and he didn't even walk it out. He came up the alley and almost run me down. Didn't even bother to look at me. Jumped off his horse and boiled into the back door of the Pink Petticoat. That's how the gents get up to the girls when they don't want everybody to see them. I had the job of walking out his damn horse, and when he came back he didn't even give me a nickel. Told him I walked the nag, and he kicked at me and walked up Main Street."

"Who was the kid?"

"Don't recall, but I might know in the morning."

"You have a good sleep and try to remember. You think on it, it could be worth a dollar to you."

"A whole dollar? I ain't seen one of them for a spell."

Spur showed him out and sat looking at the wall. He had heard about the hunting death. He'd have a talk with the sheriff about it. Then he had to take a ride on up north and see the Haworth clan. Another busy work project. But he had to do it, to relax the situation if he could. If thirty guns at both ranches started a range war he never would find out who slaughtered those stage coach people.

Spur gave Ty Udell five dollars and told him to go get a good meal and to watch around town for the two men he had seen before.

Five minutes later Sheriff Quigley had the paper in his hands.

"Yes, this is the report on the hunting death. They claim their friend shot himself when he dropped his pistol and it went off."

"That sounds a little strange. Most men carry their six-guns on an empty chamber so that sort of thing can't happen."

"True. They were so open about it that day and so shook up that I believed what they said without question. Of course, that was before we knew about the massacre." He studied the three names on the paper. "Jim Darlow was one of them, the other one was Zack Kinsey. He's the one who is dead. The third man is Roger Olsen.

"As I remember they were drinking buddies. Hang around the saloons on Saturday and by Saturday night they get into some kind of a fracas. Never anything to get arrested for."

"They work anywhere?"

"Kinsey was a hand at the Box H Haworth ranch. I think Olsen worked for the blacksmith here in town. And Darlow is out of work. Had been with one of the smaller ranches but they had to let him go. He didn't hook up with another outfit yet. Said he was looking."

"Let's just suppose, Sheriff. Just suppose the three were on that robbery, and Zack gets himself gut shot by a couple of pistol rounds. The other two go crazy and shoot everyone dead and then get their senses back. Wouldn't it be smart to bring Zack right into your office and say he was killed hunting? No cover-up on him because he's damn well dead. Could have happened that way."

"Could have, but I don't think these two have the guts or the brains to do it. I'll watch them and keep looking."

"Good. I talked with Efrem Longley this morning. The river is getting damn low and he's worried. Thought I'd ride up to see Haworth and remind him about basic water rights of downstream landowners."

"Good, we don't need a range war."

Spur waved and got back to his horse. He had stopped for a cold beer at the Pink Petticoat, but Claudine wasn't working yet.

An hour later he rode along the river on the far side, which should be the Box H land. He was looking for the sluice gate and the water works that would let Haworth capture a whole river. That would take some engineering.

He found it two miles above the end of the Longley range. The small stream took a sharp bend around a rocky point and the current swept entirely to the near side of the bank. Posts had been driven into the riverbed and a crude but effective baffling wall of three-inch thick planks had been built out over the twenty foot wide main course of the water. Over the wall was the sluice gate. It was simply another twenty foot wall of planks that cold be dropped straight down into the water and effectively block off ninety percent of the river's flow. He looked at the side of the stream and saw where a ditch had been dug. It was ten feet wide and three feet deep. The channel side was reinforced with cut logs.

It would be an effective way of diverting most of the water. Ahead along the ditch he saw what had once been a lake. Now the area was only damp with a few water plants and reeds growing. The lake could hold a large amount of water since it was in a natural catch basin that could be filled sixty or eighty feet deep.

Spur turned his horse along the ditch when a rifle bullet spanged off a rock ahead of him and whined off into the sky.

"Hold it, Buster. Right there. Not another step!"

Spur saw a horse and rider come out of the brush fifteen yards to his side, a rifle tracking him.

"Who the hell are you and what do you want?" the cowboy demanded.

Spur hadn't seen him before.

"My name is Spur McCoy. I'm a federal law officer and I want to see your boss, Henry Haworth. Now put down that weapon before I charge you with aggravated assault and throw you in the territorial prison."

The rifle lowered.

"Federal? A U.S. Marshall?"

"No. A lot higher up than that. Now take me to your ramrod wherever he is."

The rider wavered. Then nodded. "Can't take you, but I'll show you." He gave directions and Spur turned and rode north again along the valley and then up a small hill and down the other side to where a huge spread nestled next to the sparkling Santiam. There seemed to be more water in the river up here than lower down.

From this vantage point the home place of the Box H looked half again as big as Longley's. More barns, more corrals, more bunkhouses. The ranchhouse was massive, built of native stone and logs. It looked like it could stand for two hundred years. He was a mile from the spread when a cowhand rode up and asked who he was and what he wanted.

When he told him the hand called Spur "sir," and led him up to the ranchhouse and Henry Haworth. The rancher was almost as tall as Spur, but not as solid. He was fence rail thin, with deepset, brooding dark eyes, scraggles of dark hair on his mostly bald head, and clean shaven. He wore brown pants with suspenders and an undershirt with a brown sweater over it. He coughed as he looked up at Spur when his wife brought him to the study door.

"Who the hell is he?" Haworth asked his woman.

"His name is Spur McCoy, he's a federal law enforcement man and he wants to talk to you."

"Talk, about what?" Haworth said looking at Spur. The ranch owner remained seated behind a battered desk with a fancy lamp burning over it.

"Water."

"I was here first, I can use all the damn water out of the Santiam I want to."

"Not in this territory, Mr. Haworth. In the absence of any territorial water rights laws, federal law prevails."

"Who the hell says so?"

"The U.S. Constitution, the U.S. Supreme Court, and the Federal Judiciary. Do you want to fight all of them?"

Haworth looked at his wife, a small gray haired woman gone to fat years ago, and she scuttered out of the room.

"No water problems," Haworth said. "Nobody got any cattle dying of thirst."

"Not yet. But the flow of the Santiam is low, as you know, and the springs are drying up which means it's going to get lower. While I'm in the area, I want to be sure you understand the riparian rights of the land owners bordering the same flowing stream."

"Don't need to know. I do what I got to do and let the lawyers worry about it later. I let a thousand head of cattle die and then go to the law? Not a chance. I keep my beef alive whichever way I can. Then if the law comes, it comes. Dead beef don't help nobody."

"And a lot of your beef will be dead if you wind up in the federal prison for five years. Let me refresh your memory on water rights law. You have eleven ranchers downstream. Each of those ranchers has as much right to the water of the Santiam as you do. Each rancher has a right to drinking water for his cattle and his hands. If there isn't enough for everyone, for every cow, then each rancher must lose the same percentage of his herd. If that doesn't happen in a crisis situation, triple damages plus punitive damages will be assessed by the courts."

"You don't say."

"No, *I* don't say. The United States Government and the Territorial authorities say. These riparian rights are basic to our nation's welfare, and the United States Supreme Court has upheld them. What it comes down to is that sluiceway you have set up. When there is plenty of water you can use it all you want. When there isn't enough, your use of that gate will put you in direct violation of the law."

Spur was aware of others coming into the room. When he turned around, three large men stood behind him. They were as tall as their father but fifty pounds sturdier. It was plain they were the man's sons, they had his unmistakable brand.

"Hear that, boys. We got to share our river with them upstarts downstream. Like hell we will."

The oldest of the trio frowned. "We better go easy on taking that water, Pa. The law is the law, no way we can beat it."

"That's my eldest, Abel. Got a streak of logic in him that I'm trying to break. Other

91

two boys are Lot and Cain. My wife had a religious streak when she named them. Me, I just got a mean feeling. I take care of my own up here on the Box H. Anybody got any complaints they best come well heeled to talk to me about it. Right, boys?"

Cain grinned and patted the .44 on his hip. Lot said nothing and Abel frowned.

"Mr. Haworth. Let me tell you about one case in Wyoming. The court calls it a precedent, and lots of times they base their cases on past ones. Ranchers damned up a small river, cutting off all water to those below. The first drought year more than 50,000 head of cattle downstream from him died for lack of water. The rancher was fined $40 a head for the cattle, that's $200,000, and was sentenced to ten years in the federal penitentiary. He had to sell his ranch and everything he owned to pay the fine. He'll be out in five more years. Gives a body something to think about, doesn't it?"

"Get off my land, McCoy."

"Your land? I understand there is some question about how much of the Box H you really own. That's what I'll be checking into next. You have a pleasant day now."

Spur turned his back on the still seated rancher and his three sons and walked out of the room. As Spur mounted up, he saw another horseman coming toward him. He was the eldest son, Abel.

"Thought I'd ride with you out toward the gate," Abel said.

92

"Good. I'd hate to get accidentally shot by a falling six-gun." Spur watched the man but saw no reaction.

Halfway to the big gate over the entrance to the ranch, Abel said what he had come to say.

"Don't take for gospel what Pa says. He gets riled up real easy, but he don't really want trouble. He's just had to push so long to keep the place together that he's still pushing."

"I understand. But if that sluice gate drops, all the Haworths are in trouble. You remember that."

"Do my best, Mr. McCoy. Do my best."

Spur waved and rode away toward town. He should get there before suppertime, and he was hungry enough to eat half a hog.

# Chapter Nine

After his supper at the hotel, Spur went over to the Pink Petticoat to talk to Claudine. She was at the bar telling stories and waved when Spur came in. She had finished a tale about a bear and an Indian and moved down the bar to a spot beside the federal lawman.

"Nice of you to stop by again so quickly," she said, that angry smile on her face that he remembered from Arizona.

"I came and you were busy. No need for us to fight. You know my work always has first call."

She sighed, the angry smile faded and she touched his arm. "Damnit, I know. Why aren't you a saloon bouncer? I could offer you a job."

"Tried it, I didn't like it. Met both the Longleys and the Haworth families today."

"High society. Highest we got hereabouts."

"Has the weather been as dry around here as it looks?"

"Drier. We have a fist fight a week over the water rights when the river runs dry. Hope we don't have one tonight. Three of the down river ranchers are here, and then there's Cain

Haworth. That's the terrible mix. I must be a bad hostess to include them all on the same guest list. Cain's not blessed with a good temper."

"Who are the down river ranchers?"

She pointed them out to him. They were in the same poker game with six other players at a double table. Their names were Westcheski, Tsalles and Rudolf.

"They don't get into town often, but when they do, things can start to happen."

"Why?"

"They hate the big ranchers because they are small fry and the big ones are big. Lot of that going around."

"Old timers tell me this is as dry as it was three years ago," Spur said.

"They also say if it doesn't rain good and hard within a week, the Santiam will be a sandbox for the kids to play in."

"That soon?"

"They say so." She smiled. "I have to stay moving, and try to keep the beasts happy. You going to be busy later?"

"Never turn down an invitation. About midnight?" She nodded and moved down to a white-haired man at a poker table and kissed his bald head. Everyone at the table broke up laughing. Claudine knew how to keep her clients happy.

Spur walked toward the poker game with the three ranchers and saw it breaking up. The men had evidently lost a few dollars.

They moved to another table and ordered beers and sat talking. The tallest, Westcheski, was already more than a little drunk. His voice rose.

"Hell, I don't care if the little fart hears me. I still say we got just as much right to water out of the Santiam as his big outfit does."

"Yeah, sure, we agree. We just come in tonight for a good time, remember?"

"What's a good time? Hell, for me that's heading up stream with about two cases of them new fangled dynamite sticks and blow his sluice gate to old Billy hell!"

"Can't do that. Illegal." They all laughed.

Spur saw someone stand up at a poker table, then sit down when it was his turn to bid. The man was Cain Haworth and he looked mad.

Rudolph, the smallest of the three, lifted his mug of beer.

"Toast, toast to the damn weather. May it rain today, hail tonight, and wash us all into the gullies by morning!"

"Hear, hear!" somebody else shouted.

"I'll drink to that!" another voice said.

The three downed a swallow, and Tsalles stood.

"A toast to rain, and let it fall on everyone else but the Box H ranch!"

The three ranchers cheered and lifted glasses and drank. Then they roared with laughter.

Spur saw Cain start to rise, then sit down.

"I still say we should ride up there tonight, blow them guards away from that damn sluice gate and blast it to hell!" Westcheski shouted. He turned to the other men.

"Hey any of you guys with me? Who wants to get some powder and go up the river and blow up that damn sluice gate? Just dynamite it into Lincoln County!"

A dozen liquored voices rang out in the affirmative. It was the same group who would cheer if it were announced that every man who yelled loud would get his balls cut off. Spur knew the group; more important to him was Cain Haworth's reaction.

Cain pushed his chair back slowly, stood, adjusted his six-gun and walked toward the three men at the table.

"I'll go," he said. "I'll even show you where it is—then I'll blow your goddamned brains out!" Before any of the three could move, Cain's six-gun flashed into his hand and covered them.

"Now, what was this big talk about blowing up something?"

The men looked at each other. At last Westcheski pushed his chair back, stood and started to turn, then threw the chair with surprising speed at the gunman. The heavy chair caught Cain on the side as he turned away from it. It staggered him, but he kept his feet and the gun.

"You're Westcheski, the dumbassed white Russian. You run maybe two hundred head and don't know your balls from little green onions. What else you got to say?"

Spur didn't see her move. But all at once Claudine was behind Cain with a two barreled .45 deringer in his back. He felt the pressure and looked over his shoulder.

"No gunplay in here, Cain," Claudine said. "I keep telling you that. You want to stay here or ever come back, you hand your iron to the closest man. Otherwise you walk carefully out the front door and don't ever walk in here again. I can put both slugs right through your spine before you can get a shot off, and you'll be dead before you break in half. Do it now, Cain, now!"

There was a fire in her voice that Spur had never heard. Cain folded like a naughty boy, handing the .44 over his shoulder barrel first. She took it and nodded.

Cain stepped aside. She stared at West-cheski. "Rancher man, you broke up a three dollar chair. Pay up, now."

She took two steps toward him to keep him away from Cain, accepted the three silver dollars and slipped the handy little deringer back in the pocket of her flouncing skirt.

"Excitement is over, men," she said. "Back to the good stuff like drinking and playing poker."

"And women!" somebody called out.

"The best girls in the west, right upstairs," Claudine trilled, and every laughed.

Not quite everyone.

Cain Haworth glared at Westcheski. Then he charged. He caught the big Russian just as the man looked up, clamped his arms around his chest and blasted Westcheski across the table and into the next one. The jolt of the landing broke Cain's grip and he came up swinging. A right fist into the older man's gut, then one on his nose. By that time the rancher was tuned to the game.

The Russian hammered Cain's face twice, one blow on his cheek, the second one smashing his nose and bringing a gout of blood spattering the floor.

Cain bellowed in rage and bent to his boot. He pulled a six-inch knife from a boot sheath and held it in his right hand in front of him.

Spur darted in from the side, shouted at Cain, and when he turned, the agent kicked with his right foot. Leather met wrist and loosened the knife which fell to the floor. Spur stepped on the blade and stood there. He had pulled the force of the kick so it would not break Cain's wrist.

"You started it with fists, youngsters," Spur said. "You want to finish it, you do it the same way."

Cain glared at Spur, then the savage, wild gleam faded from his eyes. He shook his head and nodded.

"Yeah, sure. I'll go outside if he wants to."

The older man shook his head. "We've both been drinking too much. Maybe some other day, just you and me, kid."

"I'll be ready, anytime, old man."

Cain turned, picked up his hat and his six-gun from Claudine and marched up the stairway.

"Some poor pussy is gonna get a workout tonight!" a wag called out and everyone roared.

Westcheski looked at Spur, waved and sat back down at the straightened table. The three talked quietly, then the short rancher walked up to Spur.

"We thank you. We don't fight with knives. We all could have been cut up right bad."

"Fair is fair," Spur said. He watched the small man. "And I should warn you, I'm a federal peace officer. I don't want to hear any more talk about dynamiting any property that isn't your own."

The small man smiled. "Mr. McCoy, your work is known. We would not think of talking any more about blowing up the sluiceway or the gate. You know we have rights to the water. The next you hear from us we will already have blown up the gate, but you will not be able to prove it." He turned and went back to his friends. A few moments later they left the saloon. Spur guessed they would be on their way back south to their ranches. Dynamite wasn't for sale at night, even in High Prairie.

Claudine tapped his arm.

"Thanks. I don't like knife fights in my place either."

"You could have handled it. I was just closer."

She smiled. "I might have at that. You had supper?"

"Yep. But the right kind of snack would be interesting."

"You'll have to wait for that. Play some poker, lose some money, your public will like that."

Spur found an empty chair at a four hand table where none of the participants wore a tie. In three hours he lost four dollars, and made three friends. It was a worthwhile tradeoff.

By twelve-thirty the drinkers and gamblers had gone home, and only four of the girls upstairs were working. Spur helped Claudine and Barry the barman close up. They left one light on the back stairs for the late night leavers, and went into Claudine's apartment.

"How long did it take you to fix it up this way?" Spur asked.

"About a year. I've been here for almost three. Want to hear how I went from dancehall girl to saloon owner?"

'If it's a short story."

"Short and expensive. I landed in Tucson after we parted in Arizona and met a man I liked and he didn't care who or what I was, he wanted to marry me. So he did, and we stayed in town and he worked his mine and had just got it on a paying basis when he took sick. The lead poisoning came from the

101

six-gun of a rival for the same vein a hundred feet underground. Either my husband or the other man had his tunnel dug crooked. Will died a week after he was shot underground. Nobody ever knew who pulled the trigger.

"I had some friends there after six months, and they arranged a sale of the holdings. I got forty-three thousand dollars for it. More money than I thought even banks had.

"I bought some clothes, got a trunk and started hunting for a situation, a town, and a place where nobody knew me. Here I am. I am the widow of a saloon owner. That's how I learned the business. The nice ladies of the town won't talk to me. They cross the street when I come by, leave the store, but half of them have husbands who patronize the girls upstairs once a week. So I maintain my smile and my good nature, and hope and pray that Spur McCoy will find me. Damnit, an answered prayer. What the hell am I supposed to do now?"

Spur laughed softly and kissed her. "If you have any good wine and some cheese, we could try some. I hear that's all the rage in Washington and New York."

"Let's try it."

They did.

When the wine had been sampled and the cheese cut and tasted she kissed him and sat back on the edge of the big bed.

"Do you think we should make love before,

or after the bottle of wine is gone?"

"Both," Spur said.

They did.

# Chapter Ten

Barry the barkeep at the Pink Petticoat told Spur about it at 8:30 the next morning. He had just finished the breakfast Claudine had cooked for him and came into the saloon to head for the sheriff's office.

"Some Jasper rode in this morning half dead and burned bad. Doc fixed him up. He told the sheriff that some wild men had burned him out last night. Guy's name is Young and he's a rancher out about four miles north."

Spur asked Barry to tell Claudine that he would be at the sheriff's office and hurried to the little courthouse. Sheriff Quigley was almost ready to leave.

"Don't see how this has anything to do with the massacre, so I wasn't going to look you up. Welcome to come along if you want. We're leaving now. Young is still getting patched up, but he said he saw a red glow in the sky to the east of his spread. Might be a second rancher burned out last night. I don't figure where we're going I can make it by buggy, so I'm on this damn horse."

Spur ran for the livery stable and saddled

up the same horse he had used before. He caught them a mile out of town. The sheriff knew little else.

"Young said he woke up when he smelled smoke. Half the house was on fire and the barns were both almost burned down. At least he drove the horses outside and didn't lose any of the stock. He's got a wife and three kids, but they are all unhurt. He went back into the house to get a strong box with all of his cash in it. Saved it, but burned both his hands, his face and his legs. That's about it?"

"Haworth?"

"Could always be Haworth. Both these ranchers are just below the land he claims. He could be wanting to move in on them and buy them out cheap, or just run them off. Hard telling with a man like Haworth."

"That would make two fewer ranchers needing water out of the Santiam."

The sheriff nodded.

They had ridden at a trot most of the way. A quarter horse can cover six miles in an hour at that pace, and they got to the ranch a little after 9:30.

A woman rushed out from a small building near the well, her face a mask of fear.

"Is he all right? My husband got into town didn't he?"

"Yes, Mrs. Young, he's fine. Doc Varner is taking good care of him. He'll be along later with some supplies in a wagon, and some help."

Spur rode around the still smoldering, charred remains of the house, two barns and a shed. There was no way anyone could prove they had been torched. No kerosene cans, not witnesses, but there was no doubt in his mind how it had happened. He got off his horse and checked for horseshoe prints. He found several around each of the buildings, which wasn't unusual. It would make it too simple if he could find a broken shoe, or some strange markings, but there were none. Half the horses in Montana could have made the prints.

Back at the well house he talked to Mrs. Young.

"We didn't hear a thing but the fire. Woke us up and we ran out of the house. Then my husband went back in for the strong box. He was afraid the paper money and our homestead certificate would burn up even though it was in the metal box."

"He was right, it would have," Spur said. "This was a hot fire. You didn't hear or see anyone? You didn't hear any hoofbeats of horses riding away?"

"No. Must have been three or four of Haworth's men out there, but didn't see them."

"Why do you say Haworth's men?"

"He done it. My husband says so. And he's threatened us twice. Said sell to him or move out. That was it. Sell to him or move out or we'd be sorry we didn't."

"When did he threaten you?" Sheriff Quigley asked.

"Spring, when we was rounding up our strays over on the edge of his land. Said he owned the land all the way into town. My husband said we had proved up on our homestead, we owned it. He threatened us, and shot over our men's heads."

The sheriff was making notes on a pad of paper.

"Mr. Young said he thought he saw a glow to the east," the sheriff said. "Could that be over by the Foland's spread?"

"Husband said he thought it was. Good Lord, I pray that none of them got hurt." She reached her arms around the three children who huddled near her. They were from six to eight years old. "Her younguns are much smaller than ours."

Spur and the sheriff rode toward the Foland spread a half hour later. They had salvaged one bed from the remains of the house and set it up in the little well house. The kitchen stove would be salvageable after it cooled off a little more. The oldest boy had been looking for food they could still use from the root cellar and the pantry. They could eat for a few days and by then Spur was determined to have help for them.

They paused at a little rise and looked down into a feeder stream to the Santiam. The John Foland spread was smaller than the

Young place. It might run three hundred head of cattle and had a stand of corn growing in a fertile valley stretched out near the stream. Spur could see how some of the water from the creek had been diverted to feed the corn which was tall and green and starting to tassel out.

The ugly black scars showed plainly. The barn and house were charcoal and charred timbers. They could see a lean-to that had been built of partly burned boards under a tree near a windmill.

As they rode up a man came running out and fired a shot into the air.

"Hold it right there!" the man bellowed.

"John, it's Sheriff Quigley. We've come to help you."

The man put the rifle down and sank to the ground. When they came close enough they saw he was crying, tears dripping down his cheeks, his shoulders shaking with sobs.

"Jody died," the man said.

"John, is Jody your son?" the sheriff asked.

A woman came from the lean-to. She still had black smudges on her face and arms. Her skirt had been blue, now it was charcoal black. She walked up quickly and looked at her husband sitting in the dirt, the rifle leaning upward on his shoulder. He was crying, looking at the ground.

"He's been that way since Jody . . . passed on. We tried to find Jody in the dark last night. But the fire was roaring and he must have got scared and crawled under his bed. Just couldn't find him. Last few seconds John dragged me out of the room and then the roof fell in. John saved my life last night."

Spur motioned for the woman to come to one side where her husband couldn't hear.

"Might be best to bury the boy, right now. Help your husband get over his grief. Lots of times that helps the survivors."

"Yes. The Sheriff is here so it will be official. We'll do it. I'll tell John, then get little Jody ready. He was just four years old."

Spur spent the next half hour digging a grave near an apple tree. Jody had loved the apple tree his mother said. Spur jammed and slashed at the dirt, taking his anger out on it as he dug the three-foot deep hole. It didn't have to be very long.

John Foland seemed to rouse himself and take more interest as the little service began. Nicole, his wife, spoke some memorized passages from the Bible, including the Twenty-third Psalm. Spur started to lay the boy in the grave, but John shook his head and put the sheet wrapped body gently into the hole. Then as his wife prayed, he filled it in, not allowing Spur to help. He nailed together a wooden cross and mounded the dirt and pushed it in. Then John Foland blew his nose, wiped the tears from his eyes and walked over to the sheriff.

"I know who killed my boy, Sheriff. I saw them. Last night I had to get up and go to the privy. I was just coming back when I saw the barn start to burn. I ran out there and saw two men getting on horses. The horses both had Box H brands on their hips, and I'd recognize the men. They didn't know I seen them.

"I tried to put out the barn, and while I was out there they set the house on fire. Damn them! Time I got back to the house Nicole was up and waking the kids. We got four and they a handful sometimes.

"But then we couldn't find . . . I know the men, Sheriff. I can point them out in a crowd."

"Good, John. Good. We'll get things settled down here. You have a fine lean-to over there. We'll put some sides on it and see what kind of food you have left. Then we'll ride on out to the Haworth place."

They stayed there two hours. Spur found more boards and he got two sides on the lean-to. They salvaged a few blankets from the house. Soon it would be cool enough to find pots and pans. Even with the handles burned off they could be used.

Spur dug out tools and a few implements that had lasted. They could eat the sweet corn in another few weeks and had a big garden near the stream.

"Leastwise we still have the cattle," Foland said. "Tomorrow I'll drive three head in and see if I can sell them in town. I can butcher them out right there. Maybe keep one in the ice house for a while."

Spur watched Foland. He was a man back from the grave. He had suffered the ultimate torture, the death of his small son, and had mourned his heart out. Now he was healing, and while he would never be whole again, he was coming back, thinking ahead, making plans. He would survive.

They had to ride west to the Santiam, then only a half mile to the guard near the big gate. The guard scowled at the sheriff but let them through. He fired two shots into the air with his rifle to let the home place know company was on the way.

Spur had made sure that Foland did not have a gun. The odds were high that Foland would shoot first and talk later. The three rode the last half mile up to the ranchhouse and tied up their horses at the rail. As they did Haworth and one of his sons came out a side door and walked toward them.

"Sheriff, this is a pleasure. You don't get out this way much." Haworth didn't sound as if he meant it.

"Harry, you know Foland and McCoy, here."

"Yes." The rancher's eyes lingered on McCoy a minute, then moved to Foland. "Thought I saw a red glow down your way last night."

"My barn burned to the ground," Foland said.

"That's too bad."

"Thanks for sending someone over to help as soon as you saw the fire," Foland spat back at him. "Nice and neighborly."

"Wasn't sure it was your place. All my men were sleeping."

"Two of them wasn't. I was up late last night, Haworth. I saw two of your men set fire to my barn. While I tried to put that out they set fire to my house."

"Can't be true, none of my men would do that."

"Not unless you ordered them to."

"We tracked the two arsonists right here to your place," Spur said. "You've got some explaining to do."

"It's all a lie. This man has hated me for years."

"From what I hear, he has cause. We want to see all of your hands, Haworth. Those here at the place right now. Call them together."

"Afraid I can't do that. These men have work to do."

"So do I, Haworth," Spur said, drawing his Colt and training it on the two Haworths. The youth beside his father was Lot, the undecided. "You'll round up your men within five minutes, or you will be coming to town in shackles under arrest."

"You've got no jurisdiction . . ."

"The hell I haven't!" Spur thundered. "The whole damn *nation* is my jurisdiction. Lot, get the men rounded up in the mess hall. Right now."

Lot never looked at his father, he turned and walked toward the barns.

"Lot! You come back here!" Haworth thundered. Lot never broke stride.

Ten minutes later fourteen hands were in the mess hall, talking and laughing about the break in the day's work. Spur quieted them.

"The first three men, right here, stand up and move against the wall by the door and face forward."

"What the hell for?" one man asked. He was small and wiry, face burned brown but with a white forehead where his hat came. He was an outdoors cowboy.

"Because if you don't I'll knock you down and kick the shit out of you!" Spur shot back. The three man moved against the wall. Foland sat on a bench by one of the tables looking hard at the men.

"Now turn to your right, all three." The men did.

Foland shook his head. Three more men moved into position and did the same thing.

When the third group lined up Foland grabbed a tableware knife off the bench and lunged forward at the center man in the line. Spur caught him and took the knife away.

"That's one of them," Foland said. "Let me go! I'll kill the fucking bastard!"

Bolan held Foland and shook his head. "Let the law take care of it." He looked at the man. "You, step over here and sit down. You move a foot off that bench and I'll put a pair of .45 slugs right through your left eyeball. Understand?"

113

The man nodded, his bravado suddenly gone.

The other men were cleared by Foland. Spur turned to Haworth. "Where are the rest of your men? We need to screen them too."

"What about Gallagher? You charging him with arson?"

"Yes, and he'll also be charged with murder. Jody Foland died in the fire."

Haworth's eyes closed, then he squared his shoulders. "My man didn't have anything to do with that fire. We have witnesses who will swear he was here."

Spur scowled and the anger seeped out of his pores. "I bet you will, Haworth. You can buy witnesses to say any damn thing you want to. They are prejudiced and we'll prove it. Gallagher and the man he rode with are going to hang for killing that boy. He was only four! What would you have done if somebody killed one of your boys when he was four years old?"

Haworth turned and walked slowly toward the ranchhouse. The farther he got from them, the lower his shoulders sagged.

Lot came up and said they could ride down to the south pasture one ridge over where most of the other hands were branding late spring calves.

Sheriff Quigley moaned, then shrugged and got on his horse. He said he would be saddle sore for a month.

At the next valley, they found the branding

fire smoke and homed in on it. Ten men were finishing the branding. A rough corral had been built that held fifty head of calves, some of them still bawling for their mothers. A hundred head of cows bawled and stomped around the enclosure.

One by one the calves were hauled from the pen, thrown and held on one side as the Box H iron, red hot from the fire, seared the burn mark through hair and into cowhide. The bawling calf jumped up and ran into the herd of cows, hunting its mother.

Lot rode ahead and talked to the men. They stopped the branding and gathered near a water bucket. Foland rode past the men, turned his mount and came back. Halfway down the line he jumped off his bay on one of the cowboys. Foland clawed at the man's eyes, then slammed a hard fist into his nose twice before Spur got there and pulled him away.

The cowboy sat on the dirt, his chaps sprinkled with blood, his face surprised.

"That one?" Spur asked.

Foland could only nod. He kicked out viciously slamming his boot into the cowboy's leg. "That one!" Foland said. "He's the one who torched the barn."

Spur took the man out of earshot and glared at him. "I'm a federal law officer. I need to ask you a few questions. Answer them as truthfully as you can." The cowboy nodded.

"What's your name?"

"Ewald, Ed Ewald."

"How long have you worked for Haworth?"

"Near four years now."

"You good at obeying orders?"

"Long as they make sense."

"Where were you last night?"

A frown touched the man's face. He shrugged. "Playing poker with the boys. Lost two dollars at penny ante."

"Were you at the Foland ranch last night?"

"Hell no."

"That's enough for now, Ewald. You're under arrest for the murder of Jody Foland."

"That's crazy. I never even seen the guy."

"He's a child, Ewald. Four years old. He died in the fire last night when you torched the Foland's house."

"Died?"

"Right, as in dead." Spur tied the man's wrists behind his back, put him on his cattle pony and led him back to the Haworth ranch.

Lot went into the house.

Five minutes later Lot came out, said he would ride into town to arrange for a lawyer. Both the suspects were tied to their mounts and the small party rode off.

Spur talked to Foland where he turned off to his place.

"We'll have some help out to your ranch tomorrow morning. Don't worry, Haworth is paying for everything, he just doesn't know it yet."

Tears welled up in John Foland's eyes, but he kept them from spilling over.

"Thanks, McCoy. Thanks for not letting me kill either one of them murderers. That'd make me just like them. I don't want that. I got a wife and three more kids. Responsibilities. Lots of work I got to do. First got to get a house for them."

"That's what we'll help with tomorrow," Spur said.

"Much obliged, McCoy. I mean that. High time somebody put the running iron to Henry Haworth's high handed ways. He burned out one outfit north of him three years ago. Nothing was ever done. Now Haworth is grazing that land, using the pens, and the water."

"He's not getting away with it this time."

Foland nodded. A glint came in his eyes. "Damn right he ain't! Don't worry about me. I won't touch him. We got some law here now to handle him."

Spur turned and caught up with the rest hoping he could make good on John Foland's expectation.

# Chapter Eleven

Halfway to town from the Box H spread, Spur McCoy pulled the small troop to a halt and glanced over at the sheriff.

"Make a bet with you, Sheriff. I wager that both of these Jaspers are going to be shouting their heads off about how they were just following orders, that Henry Haworth is just as guilty as they are, that he ORDERED them to burn out both those ranches."

"What odds?" the sheriff asked, picking up on the ploy.

"Give you five to one."

"Fine odds, you know something I don't?"

"Peers as how, Sheriff. We got ourselves two killers, here. One would be enough. What would happen if one of these Jaspers got shot up trying to escape?"

Gallagher and Ewald looked at each other.

"Hell, you won't do that. You're a federal lawman." Ewald said it.

"Who would know?" Spur asked softly. "You might not have meant to kill that boy, but he's still just as dead. We take you into town and you got maybe one chance in ten of getting off scott free. Depending on how good a lawyer Lot here can hire. Damn, I don't like them odds."

"Which one?" the sheriff asked.

Spur shrugged. "Don't matter none to me. We could untie both of them and let the one who ran fastest get away, for a spell."

"I'd think maybe a flip of a coin," the sheriff said.

Lot Haworth frowned at both lawmen, uncertain what was going on. He had a six-gun on his hip. Neither official looked at him.

"Ewald, who told you to burn down those two ranches?"

"Nobody, damn it."

"You did it on your own? Why would you do that?"

"No, not on our own. We didn't do it."

"Think the guy who ordered a killing should have to stand trial with his bush-whackers who murdered a man on the trail?" Spur asked Gallagher.

He shrugged. "Guess so."

"Then shouldn't Henry Haworth be here beside you, getting taken to jail, charged with murder too?"

"Hell, I don't know. He just said burn them out, not kill anybody. He told us . . ."

"Gallagher, you asshole!" Ewald shouted.

"Go on, Gallagher, what else did Haworth tell you?"

The cowhand stared at his boots. "Hell, he said they were taking up space and he might have to let two hands go if the places didn't

119

get wiped out so we could get more stock in there. He said too, the water was getting shorter every day."

"So you and Ewald went out last night and torched the two ranches?" Spur asked.

"Yeah. Both."

"Which one first?" Sheriff Quigley asked.

"Young. Hell, we didn't know the kid would get hurt. We didn't mean to kill anybody! You can't charge us with murder!"

"Gallagher you slow witted cow shit!" Ewald shouted. He spurred his horse into Gallagher's mount and Gallagher fell to one side, slipped around the horse where he was tied until he hung upside down.

Spur dismounted and lifted Gallagher. As he did, Ewald took off, his horse in a hard gallop goaded on by the sharp spurs.

Lot lifted his six-gun and fired twice over Ewald's head. The cowboy stopped spurring and let the horse come to a halt. Lot rode out and brought him back.

Spur got them ready to move again. He had a confession by one man which implicated the second one. It should be enough for a conviction. Now he had to figure out how to play it against Henry Haworth. He still had a choice of charges, and he might do a little horsetrading with Haworth for a confession.

They continued on into town. Spur was still helping the sheriff book the two new prisoners, when Henry Haworth walked into the sheriff's office.

He was grim. He wore the same clothes he had on before, but now he did not have a six-gun.

Spur put down his pen and stared at the rancher.

"Your men have confessed to setting the fires. We can charge them with arson or murder. Whichever one they are charged with, you will be charged with as well. They also confessed that you ordered them to do the torchings."

Haworth took a deep breath. He pulled his hat off and slumped in a chair.

"Damnit! Nobody should get hurt in a little fire like that. I ain't admitting a thing. Fact is they could have done it themselves because I told my men I might have to lay off some hands."

"Possible," Spur said. "The government would look a lot more kindly on you, Haworth, if we knew that you had done everything you could to help those ranchers rebuild."

"How?"

"Tomorrow morning you should have two wagons loaded with food staples, blankets, clothes, kitchen gear, anything you can think of that those families might need. You send them out first thing, and you follow them up with wagons from the lumber yard taking our beams and two by fours and sheeting enough to put up two good houses.

"Could have a house raising out there

tomorrow, if we pass the word. And the Box H is going to supply all the lumber and nails and roofing and whatever they need. Right?"

The old man nodded. "Yeah, right. I ain't saying we did nothing wrong, but a neighbor got to help out. The Box H will do its part. You spread the word about two house raisings tomorrow. We need carpenters. My men don't know beans about building a house."

Spur nodded. "Can do. Now you get arrrangements made with the stores in town."

When Haworth left, Spur went up the steps to the county clerk's office and checked the deed files and the land map. He took down the descriptions based on landmarks, and then drew a crude map. From first impressions it looked as if the Box H owned about half the land they currently claimed. He would take that up with Mr. Haworth at an opportune moment.

The moment came sooner than Spur thought it would. He was in the Plainsman Hotel restaurant when Haworth came in, searched the tables until he found the Secret Service agent and walked directly to his table.

"It's done, McCoy. I gave the store instructions to put whatever they want on the wagons. One for each place. Cost me a thousand dollars before it's over. The lumber wagons will move out tomorrow and all of my hands will be split between the places to

122

help work. You should be satisfied."

"Isn't me who's trying to be pleased. I think you're trying to talk yourself into doing a good deed." Spur paused. "You checked your holdings lately with the county clerk? The land map doesn't reflect your current boundary markers at the Box H. From what I saw you own about a third of the land you have posted as yours."

"Damn lie. I own the whole thing. Bought it fair and square. Got the papers to show it."

"Did you file them with the county? Doesn't mean a thing until the paper shows up in the county clerk's office." Spur gave him the rough map. "You better take a look in your safe out at the ranch. Peers your legal ownership papers are on the shy side."

Haworth glared at Spur. "You got any more tricks up your damned sleeve? You come in here snorting and raring like a wild boar, disrupting everything."

"I didn't set any houses on fire, Haworth. I'll see you at the two house raisings tomorrow."

The gaunt, thin man turned and walked away. Something was different about him. Then Spur figured it out. His face was clean shaven.

McCoy finished his dinner and went back to the sheriff's office. The banker had found no more of the new coins. Whoever had been spending them had stopped. For a moment McCoy knew he was putting in too much time on the river war and the burnouts, but somehow it all tied together. He didn't know how, but he was going to push both ends of it. The two men who came in with their dead friend still interested him. He would talk to Claudine about them. There was a chance there might be more in the group, another one or two who hung out together, who gambled and got drunk together. It was a chance. The sheriff said he had nothing more on either Jim Darlow or Roger Olsen, but he was watching both of them.

Spur stopped at the General Store, and found them busy laying out survival gear, equipment and food for the two families. The store owner said it was the biggest order he had ever put up, but he was glad it was going to folks who needed help.

Spur began to spread the word about a pair of house raisings the next day. All able bodied men were invited to help, and their ladies could bring food for everyone. Spur hoped he could get twenty men at each site. If so they could have the houses put up and livable before darkness the next day.

He found Claudine at the bar at her saloon. He had worked all the others making the announcement about helping the burned out families. He talked about it here and heard some assurances that the men would go out. Claudine said she would take a big bunch of sandwiches, fresh fruit, and cold beer. Four more men decided to go.

Claudine led Spur to an empty poker table. "I hope you never find the killers of those stage coach people," she said softly.

"Why?"

"Then maybe you'll stay around for a couple of years looking for them."

"Might at that. Could be I won't find them."

"Promises, promises."

"What do you know about a young man named Jim Darlow?"

"Jerky Jim," that's what my girls call him. Some quaint little movements he makes in the throes of love. I don't know much more. He's around the saloon now and then. Has a few weird friends, but then don't we all? That's about it."

"He get into fights, get thrown out, rough stuff?"

"No, not any more than some loud talk. He's a big talker when he gets sloshed. You on the other hand get quiet as a bunny rabbit and exhibit certain other traits of the same species."

"Never alone."

"Never?"

"Well, almost never." He squeezed her hand. "I've got to dig up my potato patch and see what I can find. Some of the old field work. I still have a killer to find. Maybe more than one."

"I think's it wonderful what you're doing for the two families that were burned out.

Just beautiful. And I know it's you behind it. When it happened before our glorious sheriff just sniffed a little, said wasn't it a shame and did nothing."

"One hand washes the other."

"I've heard that, what does it mean?"

'I don't know what it means, I just use it." He touched her shoulder, winked and walked out into the blackness of the night.

Main Street was a dark tunnel. Only the lights from the four saloons and the hotel made any indentation in the liquid black. The rest of the stores were locked up tightly. The big Seth Thomas on the saloon wall indicated it was only a little after nine P.M.

Spur moved toward the next saloon half a block down. He had forgotten the name now and couldn't read the sign. At the alley he stepped off the boardwalk into the inch-thick dust the hooves and wagon and buggy wheels had churned since the last rain. When the next rain did come a man would be ankle deep in mud.

He was just ready to step up on the boardwalk on the other side of the alley, when a pistol in the darkness to his right fired twice. Spur felt the slug take him high in the chest, somewhere under his collar bone, and he went down and rolled, crying out when he rolled over the wounded side. His right fist was full of hardware, but he had no target.

Footsteps pounded down the alley. The Secret Service agent was on his feet at once, running after them. There was no pain in his shoulder now—not yet. Just the sudden hammer blow and then nothing. He put his right hand up and felt his shirt front.

Wet! With his blood.

He ran faster. The alley ended at the next block where there were mainly houses. He saw three lights on. Spur stopped and held his breath. Shuffling steps sounded to his left, in the side yard of the first house. He held his position and the steps came again. Spur couldn't see a thing.

Slowly his eyes adjusted and a tree took shape and beside it, staring around, stood a man. He had a pistol up. Spur leveled in and took one shot. He missed. But it flushed the man out. He ran down the dirt street between the houses. There were no boardwalks here, nor fancy curbs as in the East. Just a dirt track between the small homes.

Spur chased him, the first tinges of pain coming in his chest. The bushwhacker was not a running expert. Spur gained on him easily. The man must have known it. Suddenly he stopped, turned, held the gun with both hands and fired.

There was no time to return the fire. Spur was less than twenty feet from the gun, he did the only thing he could. The agent dove for the ground, hit on his right shoulder as he always did ready to do a neat forward roll back to his feet and keep running.

As he hit on his shoulder and his body

crushed sideways, he screeched in agony from the wound in his other shoulder. Spur couldn't complete the roll. He went down in a sprawl, lost his gun and lay there panting to stave off the light headedness he felt. He knew he was five seconds from passing out. If he did the gunman would walk up and kill him. He fought it back, took deep breaths and sat up, reaching around for his Eagle Butt Peacemaker.

Ahead he saw the gunman moving his arm, tracking Spur with the handgun. Spur moved to one side, felt the blood rush away from his head and ducked low. The shot went over his head. With his head down blood flowed back into it.

His right hand closed over the mother-of-pearl handgrips of his .45 and he whirled it around and fired. The bushwacker jumped in surprise. Spur had not even aimed. He couldn't afford the time. He was letting the man know he had his gun back. The man turned and ran.

This time Spur had trouble keeping up with him. Every step, every jolt of his feet sent small needles stabbing through his shoulder. They went down a block, cut back toward Main Street and then he saw the man was silhouetted against the lights of a saloon. Spur stopped, held the .45 in both hands and fired the last two shots in the cylinder. The second one hit the man in the leg and he toppled. He tried to stand, fell and then began dragging himself toward the alley.

Spur walked as fast as he could toward the ambusher. Two drunks came out of the bar singing to their "doggies." They turned away from the man in the dirt. Another man came out walking more steadily.

"Stop that man!" Spur shouted. "The man on the ground is a killer, stop him!" The man looked Spur's way, but could see nothing. He drew his weapon and moved cautiously toward the man who now lay still in the middle of the street.

It took what to Spur seemed like ten minutes to walk the half block to the street. Three men stood near the man in the dirt.

"Broken leg," one man said.

"Know who this Jasper is?" another asked.

"He fainted, ain't that odd?" a third voice said.

Spur came reeling up to the group and put his hand on one man's shoulder for support.

"Hey. It's that federal lawman. He's been shot!"

Spur let himself down to the ground and turned over the man who lay there.

"Who is he?" Spur asked, his head feeling light again.

"Hell, that's Jim Darlow. He's losing blood fast." The man put his kerchief over the upper leg wound.

"Better get Doc, both of you could see him."

"Darlow. Jim Darlow is under arrest,"

Spur said, then he fell backward into the arms of the man behind him and the darkness of rest closed over him.

# Chapter Twelve

Spur McCoy awoke in a small plain room. He was in bed and felt like somebody had run over him with a twelve mule team freight wagon. When he moved his left arm, pain gouged a dark hole in his brain and he groaned. Then he remembered: he had been shot.

A form appeared in the lighted doorway. He wore a white shirt with rolled up sleeves. Dark spots of blood showed on the front of the shirt. The man came into the room nodding.

"Good, glad you came back to life. Thought I'd lost you for a while there. How much blood do you think you can spread around town and still have enough to live on?" The form came closer. "I'm Doc Varner, the resident sawbones. Welcome back."

"Glad to be here. Bullet miss my lung?"

"Barely, but you bled like a stuck shoat. Your prisoner is in better condition, just a broken leg. I set it and he's over in Sheriff Quigley's boarding house."

"I hope that's a jail cell."

"It is. Quig said he wanted to see you, if you

made it. He's outside."

"He wanted my Eagle Butt Peacemaker," Spur said feeling a little woozy. He couldn't take time out to be shot. He still had lots of work to do.

Sheriff Quigley came in. "I hear you're tired of working with me," he said a wry little smile sneaking around the corners of his face.

"Hell yes," Spur said, stopped and took a deep breath.

"Jim Darlow said you shot him for no reason. Thought I better check your version."

Spur told him in short sentences, with pauses between.

"Check the alley over there, should be a blood trail down it."

"No reason to. I went to Darlow's boarding house and went through his things. He was one of the men who brought in that dead friend the day of the massacre. Under his bed, back in the corner where his landlady couldn't reach, I found a tin box. Inside were forty-six double eagles, 1873 mint date."

"Good. So he's one of them. You figure the other guy, Olsen and their dead buddy did the job?"

"Possible. Only trouble is I checked out Olsen's room here at the hotel. Nothing, not a single twenty dollar gold piece in the place. He evidently was smarter hiding them, or he wasn't involved."

Spur tried to think it through. Something

was out of place, but his head kept spinning. He tried to sit up and came within a second of passing out. At last he got the words said.

"That accidental death. They said Zack Kinsey dropped his six-gun. it went off and killed him. Did you check with the undertaker to find out if the body had just one bullet wound?"

"No, but I sure will. You take it easy. Looks like this thing is starting to wind down."

"Wish it was, but we have a lot of problems yet. You going to the house raising tomorrow?"

"Yes, in my buggy. Half the county is going to be out at those two places."

"Good. Hope I can make it." Spur wanted to say more but his eyes were too heavy and they closed before he knew it and he fell asleep.

The sheriff closed the door quietly, and talked to Doc Varner.

"Not a chance," Varner said. "McCoy is damn lucky to be alive. Another inch lower and his lung would have been hit and he'd have a lung fill up with blood where it isn't supposed to. He isn't moving out of that bed for at least three days."

Sheriff Quigley smiled. "If that's what you want, you better have some rope to tie him in. I got to pay a call on our undertaker. Seems strange going down there without a body for him to work on."

Spur woke up hungry. He forgot for a moment where he was and threw back the light cover and groaned as his left side chattered in pain.

The door popped open and Claudine bustled in.

"We thought you were going to sleep all day. Here it is after eight A.M." She stopped and a soft, gentle smile replaced the frown as she hurried to the bed and kissed his forehead.

"A fever. Doc said you would run one for three days. He had a devil of a time finding that slug and getting it out. He says we almost lost you."

"I'm too mean to die."

"Hush. I brought you some breakfast. Doc says anything, and the more the better, but no booze. Can you stand that for three days?"

"Have to."

He tried to sit up, but the waves of pain, nausea and light headedness came back. Claudine fed him with his head propped up just a little. She had brought a stack of hot cakes, hot maple syrup, two fried eggs. three slices of toast and strawberry jam, and a bowl of applesauce. He ate most of it.

"Did they get out of town on the house raising?"

"Half of town pulled out bright and early."

"I need to go."

"It's a long way to crawl. You can't ride."

"You have a buggy?"

She laughed. "Come on, Spur. You got the project started moving. They know how to do it. Heard one old timer say he hadn't seen a house raising like this in the county in thirty years."

"It's a good thing to get started again."

Spur took several deep breaths. "Yeah, that didn't hurt. Now I'm going to sit up. That breakfast helped." He wouldn't let her touch him as he edged higher and higher in the bed until he was sitting against the headboard.

"You get feeling any friskier and I'll jump right in there beside you," Claudine said.

"Don't tempt me. Where are my pants?"

Claudine lifted the covers and peeked under. "You're not wearing them, I can tell."

"Funny, Claudine, cute, strange. Find my damn pants."

"My, you *are* feeling better." She frowned slightly as she found his clothes on a chair below the bed.

By stages Spur was testing himself. He began by leaning away from the headboard. He almost fell off the bed. Again and again he tried until he could do it. He looked down at the bandage on his chest. It was high and taped in place.

After a half hour of work he could sit up without help and then began working on moving his legs over the side. That was easier.

An hour after breakfast he could walk with Claudine's help.

"Have you taken those sandwiches and beer out to the ranches yet?" he asked her.

"No. I've leaving about ten."

"I'll ride with you. Get Doc in here to wrap this damn hole in me again. I think it bled some."

When Doc Varner came in he was angry. "Tarnation! What in hell are you doing, man? Trying to kill yourself?"

"Got work to do, Doc. I remember a major in the war got a bullet through a lung. Next day he was back on the front lines directing a company of infantry. Depends on how much *want to* a man's got. Mine's pretty high right now. Bandage this hole up so it don't leak no more. I got to take a buggy ride out to the house raisings."

"Can't do it. Won't do it. You could start bleeding . . ." Doc Varner raised his brows and sighed. "What the hell, you're probably tougher than anybody I ever worked on. Sit down and take off your shirt. I ain't gonna help a strong man like you do a simple thing like remove his shirt."

"Atta boy, Doc," Spur said. The shirt was the hardest thing to take off. He left his left sleeve in and motioned for the sawbones to get busy.

When Claudine's buggy stopped in front of the doctor's office a half hour later, Spur was sitting in a chair in the sun waiting for her. Standing and getting up into the buggy tested his determination over pain. But he made it.

136

A line of sweat popped out on his forehead, but quickly evaporated. It was another hot, dry day, with not a hint of a cloud in the sky. And the river was lower again.

Claudine drove. She knew the way. The first half mile was murder on his shoulder. Then Spur began to exercise his mind-over-pain system. He tried to shut off the nerves that sent him the pain signals, and after a half hour of concentration, he had the pain dampened down to a slow rolling throb. He settled for that.

Claudine kept up a line of chatter all the way, evidently hoping to take his mind off his hurt. When they came over the last little rise and saw the Young place below, she shivered.

"Those two black things used to be a house and a barn?"

"Two days ago. Fire has a way of putting an end to lots of things."

Even from the distance they could see the activity below. It looked like a bumblebee nest. Teams of horses were dragging charred timbers away from the foundation. Wagons were loaded with the charred wreckage and hauled away. What looked like fifty or sixty people milled around, evidently working with some plan in mind.

The foundations were uncovered and the floor studs had been hammered into place by the time Claudine drove in.

It was a whirlwind of activity. Teams of men framed up stud walls. Others built triangular roof beams that would be lifted in place. There was a friendly, happy spirit everywhere. A dozen women had set up makeshift tables of boards over sawhorses, and had laid out a feast of fried chicken, potato salad, stews, meatloaf, and a dozen green salads, bowls of fruit, and the specialty dishes of half of the women in town.

One man came up and shook Spur's hand.

"I ain't seen nothing like this since back in the thirties," he said. "That was in Michigan and we had a barn raising one Sunday. We didn't have nowhere this many people. Does a body good to see this kind of outpouring of being a good neighbor."

He went back to pounding nails in the braces between the studs.

There was a whoop of excitement as the first stud wall was lifted into place. Two by four braces held it upright as the plate was nailed to the floor that had been rapidly laid over the joyce. Soon the second, longer wall was ready and hoisted up, nailed down and anchored firmly to the first one.

Before noon the four stud walls were up and the first of the framed-in rafter triangles were lifted up.

Men ate in shifts at the table, some working, others eating. Even before the final rafters were in place a team began pounding on the siding, starting at the bottom with the overlapping shiplap and working up to the top, allowing space for the men who had been framing in the doors and windows.

Spur had been walking around the yard cautiously. Claudine was next to him and now and then he had to touch her hand for support. Everyone knew he had been shot and marveled that he was out of bed.

Out near where the barn had been, Spur saw another crew at work. The plank corral had been burned, too. The half next to the barn was gone. Four men worked there, using salvaged lumber from the burned house and barn to reconstruct the enclosure.

When Spur walked in that direction he saw the ramrod on the project was Lot Haworth. Spur noticed Abel Haworth with his shirt off digging a post hole. Spur took Lot's hand in a silent greeting. Spur knew that if and when their dad moved on, the Box H would be in much better hands.

A rider came in from the Foland ranch. He reported work there was going well. They were about an hour behind the work being done at the Young place. He said they had sixty people, men, women and kids working there.

Spur tried to count. He gave up but figured there were over sixty at work here.

The cold beer, kept wrapped in burlap sacks filled with crushed ice from the community icehouse, was the hit of the house raising.

By two o'clock Spur had returned to the buggy and sat watching the roofing. There had not been enough sawed or split shingles in the lumberyard, so one side of the house was being shingled, and the other half covered with shiplap directly on the sheeting. It would hold for a year or two, but would be replaced with shingles if they arrived before winter.

"Cowboy, I'm going to take you home," Claudine said. The stone and rock fireplace was rising over the end of the house as the masons worked. There would be no fire in the box below for three days to allow the mortar to cure naturally.

Spur nodded. "Yes, I do feel a little tired."

She had saved two cold beers for him and he drank both on the way back. She drove slowly, but at every bump Spur winced. When they got back in town she turned down the alley in back of the Pink Petticoat and stopped.

Barry came from the bar and helped Spur into Claudine's bed. He sank down gratefully in the featherbed, thanked Barry and dropped off to sleep at once.

Claudine had put down his protests when he saw where she was taking him. She told him he needed nursing care, he wasn't going to be able to climb those steps to his hotel room, she had a bed and wanted to take care of him, and if he didn't like it he could shoot her. He kissed her instead and left her quivering in delight.

Now she looked down at him. Her hand on his head showed that his fever was almost gone. Now all she had to do was feed him and keep him quiet and let his strong body recuperate.

She smiled. Claudine wouldn't care if it took him two weeks to get back on his feet. But she knew she was dreaming.

# Chapter Thirteen

Spur could not get out of bed the next day. He woke up with the fever again and the doctor brought some pills he said should help bring down the temperature. He scolded Spur for going to the house raising the day before. Spur was so sick he didn't even want to talk about the case.

By evening he was feeling better and ate two steaks and had two bottles of beer. Sheriff Quigley came by just after supper with a note of optimism.

"We call our undertaker Digger here, just for fun. He doesn't seem to mind. Anyway, Digger told me this afternoon that he remembers that Zack Kinsey death. He keeps records on the cause of death, and he has it in his book as two gunshot wounds two inches apart in the lower belly slanting upward. Zack was probably on a horse and shot by someone on the ground."

"Like he was robbing a stagecoach," Spur said.

"That would be a good assumption, Mr. McCoy. At least we know the pair lied about the death. So they have to clear that up. And one of them had some of the stolen coins. So we have a definite linkup between Kinsey, Darlow and Olsen. It just depends how far we can push it. I'm hoping for a confession."

"Are you going to arrest Olsen?" Spur asked.

"Not yet. I want him to sweat a little. He knows we have Darlow. He's probably worried about what he's talking about all day long in the jail."

"Good. If he runs, he's almost signing his death warrant."

Spur offered the sheriff a bottle of cold beer and the lawman accepted. He relaxed a little and unbuttoned his vest.

"I still can't figure out why they shot all six on the coach," the sheriff said. "If one of the passengers shot up one of the robbers, why not just kill him and let the others go?"

"That's one we're going to have to ask Darlow and Olsen," Spur said.

They talked about the house raising. The sheriff had been at the Foland place, and said they got it up and closed in even to the windows and doors before dark. He said the Young house was done all except for the door and two men were going back today to hang them.

A half hour later the sheriff left and Claudine came back from showing him out the door. She stood and looked at Spur with her own brand of puzzled frown.

"You were talking about three men and the

stage. What about the fourth one?"

"What fourth one?" Spur asked. "We only know about the three who came back that day, two alive and one dead."

"Oh! I always think of them as the Big Gun Four, that's what my girls call them. These four guys run around together all the time. Or they used to before Zack got killed. They would come upstairs and have a contest for the most times in a row, say in an hour. Loser had to pay. The girls kept track." .

"Weird. Who was the fourth man?"

She walked around the room. "Hell, I guess there aren't any professional ethics here. They do lots of things together, like go buck hunting, and antelope hunting. Yeah, I can tell you. The fourth man on the Big Gun Four is Cain Haworth."

Spur looked at her for a long moment. Then nodded. "He's the Jasper who tried to knife those ranchers the other night. I'd say he has a violent temper. What do the girls say?"

"He's a steady with one, Pauline. She does get black and blue now and then. It's a rule, they always have to tell me if a customer gets rough. Most of her bruises come from Cain. He's a no good bum as far as I can see. But his mother probably loves him!"

"That fits in nicely. Where was Cain the day of the massacre? That is the question we need to find out. Did Pauline get any bruises that day?"

"I keep records. I can damn well tell you." She went to her desk in the other room and came back with a small leather bound book. "Fact is she did. Pauline said Cain was here most of the day."

"The day? Your girls work during the day?"

"Not usually. He could have been here. Let me look up the cash pay records." She came back with a red leather bound book. "I'll be damned. It shows Pauline had a twenty dollar customer for most of the day on July 22. That was the same day as the massacre."

Something was pricking his memory. Something about that same day. One of the men who came in response to his posters around town. Then he remembered. The drunk who said some wild eyed man almost rode him down in the alley. The man got off his half dead horse and went in the back door of the Pink Petticoat Saloon and whoring place. That drunk, Spur had to find him. If he could identify the person going into the brothel and tie down the time, it could break an alibi. If the kid who rode in so fast was Cain Haworth.

"That might give us something. Can you send out somebody to find Ty Udell?"

"Sure. I see him around now and then. Why him?"

"He might be able to help us."

"Tonight?"

"Right now."

"See what I can do."

"Tell whoever you send it's worth a five dollar gold piece if he can bring Udell back with him tonight."

Claudine came back a few minutes later. "I sent out two men who need work. They'll find him if he's in town. What is this all about?"

Spur told her. "A man doesn't ride a good horse almost to the point of collapse and then let it stand around. Best way to kill a horse there is. A mount like that has to be walked out, cooled down gradually. Udell might know the name of the drunk who saw all this happen. If he does, we have a good strong nail in Cain Haworth's hanging scaffold."

Undell came to the door two hours later. Yes, he knew the name of the man with whom he had waited in the hall.

"Snuffy Norbert, that's the guy's name. I've shared a pint with him now and then."

"Can you find him?"

"Yeah, just left him at the joint down the street. Well we was kind of behind the joint down the street."

Spur flipped him a double eagle. "Go get him and bring him back here. Come in the back door. Then hang around out front and have a beer, but don't get sloshed. I might need you again."

Ten minutes later Spur looked at Snuffy. The man had been on a three day drunk. He could barely stand.

"Sorry," Snuffy said. "It was his five dollars."

"Get him into a room over at the hotel and dry him out. I want him to be talking and making sense by noon tomorrow. No booze, but all the food you can get in him. Now get him out of here. Snuffy . . . no more booze for you either," Spur told Udell.

"Right. For a month's pay I can go dry for a couple of days. He'll be dry, I can guarantee you."

"Let's have a talk with Pauline."

"She's working."

"And I'm her next customer, right here." He handed Claudine a five dollar gold piece.

"Don't spoil her, that's overpayment."

"Not for what I'm going to do. I want you to watch."

"Strange, but interesting."

Spur had Pauline sit in the chair beside his bed and he grilled her for an hour. She wouldn't change her story. Cain had been with her almost all day. He had come early in the morning. His friends had gone hunting, but he didn't feel so good and she sat with him and got some food for him. He was there when his two friends came back with the dead man. She knew because when he heard the commotion outside, he dressed and went out. She watched from the window.

"Pauline, if you're lying to protect him, I'm going to throw you in jail. You understand that?"

She nodded, biting her lower lip.

"Pauline, if you're lying, you won't be working here anymore, whether you go to jail or not," Claudine said.

Pauline looked quickly at Claudine, then nodded again. "I know. That's what happened. Why would I lie?"

"Because Cain might kill you if you didn't," Spur said.

She snapped her head up, started to say something, then hurried out of the room.

"She's lying," Spur said. "I can feel it. I know it. We've got to get some proof to show her, to implicate Cain so she'll testify for us."

"Maybe Snuffy."

"I hope Snuffy."

That night after Claudine closed up she came into the bedroom and undressed slowly. Spur watched. She came and stood near the bed, naked, and touched his shoulder.

Spur shook his head. "Maybe tomorrow. I'm doing good just sitting up, let alone trying to get anything else up."

She laughed and slipped into bed beside him. She didn't touch him, and that took a lot of effort.

"Like we were married," she said. "Can't have sex every night. Kind of like we were married."

"Don't worry, I'll make up for this lack of response just as soon as I can." He reached over and kissed her lips gently, then went to sleep.

She lay there a long time watching him. Then smiling and thinking about the next night, she drifted off to sleep.

When Claudine woke up the next morning, Spur was no longer in the bed beside her. She heard him in her kitchen. By the time she got out there he was eating ham and eggs and fried potatoes with onions.

"Want some?" he asked.

She nodded and he served her enough for three men, then went back to eating.

"Remarkable recovery," she said.

"Two days, that's all I can afford to be sick. The two days are up, so I have to get back to work. I've already walked around the block to test myself. Breakfast, then over to Doc Varner for a look at my puncture and a nice quiet chat with Roger Olsen before he decides to leave town."

"And don't forget Snuffy."

"He won't be making sense until this afternoon. Then I might also come and see Pauline. Tell her not to leave town suddenly."

Spur finished the breakfast, gulped down the last of his coffee and kissed her cheek.

"Work calls. I'll be back for that postponed romp I owe you, or you owe me, whatever."

She waved, still a little in a daze by his activity.

Doc Varner had been up for only ten minutes when Spur pounded on his door. The sawbones was surprised at Spur's appearance. His fever was gone, his balance back, and the wound was staring to heal nicely. He put some ointment on it and bandaged it up again wrapping some of the strips around Spur's chest and back.

Spur checked his six-gun as he came out the doctor's door. It was in place and working right. Not much to go wrong with a six-gun. He walked to the hotel and asked the clerk which room Roger Olsen had, and went up to 216. He tried his key and found that like many poor quality locks, his key worked just as well in the other lock.

Spur nudged the door open slowly, then standing behind the wall, pushed the door fully open. Nothing happened. He peered around the door waist high, and saw a man sleeping in his bed, fully clothed, and a six-gun inches from his right hand.

McCoy stepped in soundlessly, picked up the weapon and punched the butt into the man's stomach.

He came awake with a start, his right hand scratching for the gun that wasn't there. Olsen sat up.

"What the hell is this?"

"Judgment day, Olsen. Are you right with your Maker?"

"McCoy, the hot shot federal lawman. Heard about you."

"So did Jim Darlow, and he's in jail talking about everything he can think of. He's probably making up some of it, but right now it sounds good."

"That's his problem."

"It's also your problem, Olsen. Get up, we're going for a ride, just you and me."

"Where? The jail? You got nothing to charge me with."

"We've got plenty. Remember Darlow is our witness now."

"That sonofabitch!"

"True, but he's *our* sonofabitch. Now get smart. I'd just as soon blow your head off right now. You want to live, you forget about trying to run for it, or push somebody in my way. I never miss at ten to twenty feet. Now walk."

When Spur first started his plunge back into normality, he wasn't sure he could make it. His legs were rubbery, his shoulder ached, and a headache kept zapping him behind his eyes. But the walk around the block had started his juices flowing, and now the mental lift of getting his sights on one of the suspects lifted his physical powers as well.

Downstairs Spur told Olsen to point out his mount at the small stable behind the hotel. Spur told him to walk the horse to the livery two blocks over where Spur called to the hand there to bring out a horse saddled and ready to move.

A half hour later they were across the Santiam and moving into the drier side of the river. Ahead long rolling hills seemed to vanish into a plain. They crossed several dry water courses and Spur swore at them softly.

He found the spot he wanted, far enough

away from everyone so a shot or two and a scream would not bring any curious or helpful.

"Get off your nag," Spur told Olsen. "Dismount, right here."

Olsen got down. Spur took the reins to his horse and rode off fifty yards and tied both mounts to a struggling limb of a brushy tree.

He walked back and told Olsen to put his hands behind his back. Spur tied them with a length of rawhide he had brought with him.

"Sit down anywhere, and make yourself comfortable. This might take a few minutes."

"What?"

"You're gonna be dying to find out."

Spur kicked around some outcropping rocks nearby and soon found a rattlesnake. The reptile skittered away from him, but McCoy found a forked stick and pressed the snake into the sand with the fork behind the triangular shaped head. Deftly, the Secret Service agent picked up the rattler, holding it just in back of the head so it was helpless.

A few kicks later he found a second rattler and captured it the same way.

Olsen had watched with interest. Now he stood up and backed away.

"Hey, them things can hurt a guy."

"True, but only if they get their fangs into your flesh. Come on."

Spur prodded Olsen forward by thrusting the angry snakes toward him. Twenty yards ahead there was a dry wash, three feet deep, with steep sides. Spur kicked dirt down from the side to form a two-foot high dike on one end. Then four feet away he did the same thing, forming a small box-like earth hole.

"You ever heard of the Apache justice system, Olsen?"

"Hell no, I ain't no Indian."

"Pretend. The Apaches say that an accused man has a right to prove he is innocent. First he is asked if he wishes to confess to the charge. If he says he is innocent he is put in a pit with from two to ten rattlesnakes, depending on the severity of the charges. If he is bitten by the snakes and lives, he is declared innocent. If he is not bitten by the snakes after an hour, he is declared totally innocent.

"On the other hand, if he is bitten and dies, he is guilty. Now isn't that a simple, efficient form of justice? No bother with a jury, or a judge or a gallows. I like it. Quick, clean."

"I said I ain't no Indian."

"Right now you are." Spur dropped both snakes into the makeshift pit and watched them. They could not climb out. When they tried, the side fell down on top of them. Spur spun Olsen around and tied his feet together. Then he picked up Olsen and moved him a few feet to the pit.

"Remember, if you live, you're innocent. The roundeye courts won't be able to charge you with anything."

"Innocent of what?" Olsen said, still not

believing he was going to be put in the pit.

"Innocent of the slaughter of six people on that July 22 stage. Anything you want to say first?"

"Hell no!"

One of the snakes tried to crawl up the side, but tumbled back down. It coiled at one end, its tail rattling a defiant warning.

Spur picked up Olsen and dropped him into the pit at the end where the snake had not coiled. The pit was only four feet long, and Olsen fell on his side, then pulled his feet partly under him and tried to stand.

"You stand up I'll blow you in half," Spur said, firing one round past Olsen's head.

He screamed. The wail came out loud and plaintive, a kind of defiant plea for help and sorrow and anger all in one.

Spur threw a rock at the coiled snake and it uncoiled and glided toward the new element that had entered the pit. The rattler slithered around Olsen's pants covered leg. The suspect shivered and screamed again.

"Get me out of here!" Olsen said at last. "Get me out!"

"Were you there at the stage massacre, July 22?"

"Yes, damnit, yes! Now get me out of here!"

"Did you kill any of the six persons that day?"

"No, damnit, no!"

"Did Jim Darlow do it?"

"Christ! What do you want? I was there. Darlow was there, Zack was there. None of us done it."

The snake tried to go up the wall but the loose dirt crumbled down again. It turned and slithered straight for Olsen's exposed knee. He shivered. The rattler's eyes glittered. It stopped a foot from the foreign thing and coiled. Its rattler beat a steady warning.

Olsen looked down and saw the growing dark wet stains on his pants. He shivered.

"Well, Olsen still wets his pants. I didn't know that. Wait until I tell the girls up at Claudine's place. Who killed the people, Olsen? Who was the fourth man?"

"He would kill me."

"So will the snakes, but they'll do it right now and it will hurt a lot more. I've heard it takes about six hours after the bite. Your arm swells up to twice its size, your head almost explodes. You get so hot you think you're going to melt, and then everything goes crazy, and you babble and scream and puke all over."

The first snake had nestled in Olsen's lap. The lower tie had come loose enough so he could cross his ankles and his knees splayed out on each side. His wrists were still fastened behind him. The rattler felt the warmth of his body and welcomed it like another sun.

Olsen looked at it and screamed. His cry of fate and death and protest carried across the high prairie for half a mile before it blended with a gentle west wind and faded into the past.

"Who was the fourth man, Olsen?"

The snake behind him was still coiled, beady eyes smarting from the sand, still angry at being captured. The rattle picked up in intensity. The snake struck. Its lightning like thrust hit Olsen's foot, one fang sinking in and sticking in the rubber heel, the other fang hanging in air. It was trapped.

Olsen screamed again, but the rattler on his legs didn't seem to notice.

"Who was the killer, Olsen?"

"Cain." The name was said so softly Spur almost missed it.

"Who?"

"Cain Haworth! He went crazy. The kid from the stage pulled down Cain's mask and the driver recognized him and blurted out his name, and right then he figured he had to kill them all. Cain was a madman, screaming and shouting. I never seen a man so much like an animal. Now get them snakes out of here!"

Spur shot the first one off Olsen's boot, killing it. The second one he held down with the forked stick, pushing it off Olsen's legs so he could hop out of the way, then he let the snake go.

"What else happened up there on the trail?" Spur said.

"The driver pulled a deringer and shot Zack, and that spurred Cain on with his rifle and six gun. Then he shot all the horses and burned up the wagon. We figured if we brought Zack back saying he got accidentally shot hunting it would work. Damn near did."

"You want to hang, Olsen? According to the law you're just as guilty as Cain. You were there, you were a robber, and the deaths were a result of that robbery."

"Christ no! I didn't kill anybody! We was just out for a little fun!"

"You write out completely what happened up there, and we might be able to get you off with, maybe five years. Cain will hang, no way around that."

Olsen worried it. Spur cut his feet free and he stood.

"Damn that wild-assed crazy Cain Haworth! Should have known better than to ride with him. Crazy! Crazy as loco weed." At last he looked across the prairie. "I sure as hell don't want to hang for something Cain did. I'll testify against him. Tell it all just the way it happened. But you got to keep Cain away from me."

"Easy," Spur said. "Now I have to find Cain and bring him in."

"That might be easier to say than to do," Olsen said.

The two men walked to their horses and Spur helped Olsen mount. He left the man's hands tied, to remind him he was a prisoner, and he would be for a long, long time.

# Chapter Fourteen

Sheriff Quigley was not surprised when he found out who the fourth man on the robbery-murder was.

"Cain has been headed for the gallows for a couple of years. Thought he could do anything to anybody. Just the opposite of his two brothers."

"Sheriff, let's keep it quiet about picking up Olsen and his confession. Then we can go get Cain tomorrow. Hate to admit it but I feel a little tired."

"Tired. A normal man would be in bed recuperating. We'll get Olsen to write out exactly what he has to say and sign it. You said if he cooperated with us we would charge him just with the robbery?"

"Figured it was a good trade. If he tries to back out of it, you remind him that I will come around and rattle his head."

One short walk up the block and Spur climbed the stairs to his second floor room in the Plainsman. He unlocked the door, stepped to the side and pushed it open. Nothing happened. He went around the frame and inside.

A girl sat on his bed.

"Good morning, Mr. McCoy."

She was Bathsheba, Bee, the eldest daughter of Efrem Longley who had been so sexy in their short talk in the parlor at the Longley spread.

"I heard you were shot and I wanted to come be your nurse. I'm good at nursing."

"Yes, I bet you are."

"Come in and close the door, Mr. McCoy."

"I shouldn't do that, we're alone."

"Yes, at last!" She shrugged her shoulders and her blouse fell to the bed. Her ripe, pink tipped breasts thrust out at him invitingly. "Close the door and lock it, Spur, I need you."

"You shouldn't be doing this." He closed the door and leaned against it.

"I know. But I want to go all the way just once to know what it feels like. I told you I'd made love before. But I haven't. One of the men at the ranch teases me. Lets me play with him but he won't do it, you know, put it inside me. He says my father would kill him."

She slid off the bed and he saw she wore only drawers that had been cut off just below the crotch. She was slender, with good hips and beautiful legs. Her breasts bounced and jiggled as she walked toward him. Spur felt his hot blood surging. She touched his shoulders, then leaned against him, her beautiful breasts flattening against his chest, her arms around him.

He felt the heat of her body. Her long blonde hair tumbled around her shoulders, some falling down her chest. She looked up at him.

"Would it be asking too much if you could kiss me?"

He did. Spur was surprised by the fire, the need, the hotness of her kiss. He held it as long as she wanted him to and it burned and burned until his mouth opened and her tongue darted inside, swinging around searching for his.

When they came apart, Spur was rock hard and ready. Her hand found his erection and she squealed in joy.

"Oh, yes! This is going to be a glorious party! And nobody to worry about, and no straw poking me in the back."

Spur smiled. "The ranch hand had you in the haymow?"

"We tried, but people kept coming in the barn. I nearly died wanting him. All he did was play with my boobies."

She led Spur to the bed, sat him down.

"I know you were shot and still recuperating, so I'll be careful of you. I can be on top even."

She unbuttoned his shirt and took it off, her eyes wide at the bandage around his chest.

"Does it hurt a lot?"

"Not now." His hands touched her breasts and she gasped, then smiled.

160

"Yes! It seems so natural. It feels good."

"It's supposed to. There's nothing unnatural about sex between a man and a woman."

"Show me!"

"We have lots of time. Aren't you afraid of getting pregnant?"

"No. I just finished my . . . my bleeding. A friend of mine says a girl can't get pregnant the day after she stops. That's why I came to find you today."

He reached out where she stood over him and kissed one rosy tipped tit. She shivered. He kissed it again and then nibbled on the morsel before pulling it into his mouth.

Bee moaned and fell on the bed on her back. Her knees drew up and spread and her hips pounded up and down as she shivered and trembled and a series of six hard spasms shot through her frame, distorting her pretty face, as she gasped for breath and tightened her small hands into fists.

The climax passed and she lay there panting.

"Good lord! I've never had one like that before. My friend rubbed me one night when we stayed together, but it wasn't that fine!"

She laughed softly. "I have an idea it's just going to get better and better!"

She unbuttoned Spur's fly and then pulled off his boots and his pants. She saw his short underpants and started to pull them down, but stopped. She jumped on the bed and lay and motioned for him to follow.

Spur lay down with some pain in his chest, then she was leaning over him, her breasts dangling delightfully above him.

He pulled her forward and let one tit drop into his mouth. Bee giggled, then her color rose and she nearly climaxed again.

"Oh, god but that feels good!" She was panting again.

"Take my shorts off," Spur said.

"Yes, I want to see all of you." She knelt beside him and slowly worked the garment down his hips until his hard penis swung upward.

"Oh! Oh! My, it's so big! How could that ever go in . . ." She sat there on her feet staring. Her hand came out and touched it and it jerked. She laughed and grabbed the shaft. "So hard! Like a stick."

"The better to enter you. Mother Nature thought of the problem. You've seen horses and dogs mate."

"Yes, but not up close. So hard!"

She stripped the shorts down and was fascinated by his scrotum.

"I've never really looked . . ."

Spur waited and let her explore. When she was satisfied, he pulled her over him on his right side and kissed her. She leaned back and stared at him.

"Gosh, but you are handsome! I'll always remember my very first time!"

"You sure you should? That you want to do it?"

"Yes! I've waited too long. My friend Betty says she's glad she finally did. Now she does, every once in a while, well, every month. She has a steady boyfriend and they get away. Once out in the woods that she said was just beautiful. They were naked in the grass and the sun shining down, then they played in the stream."

"I can't give you sunshine or a river."

"I don't need that. I want this bed and you!"

He put his hand on her round bottom and massaged it. She still had on the cut off drawers. His hand worked around and lower until he was massaging between her cheeks.

"Maybe we should take off the rest of your clothes."

"Maybe."

"You can always back out."

She sat up at once and stripped off her drawers, then turned and straddled his stomach. He was staring at her blonde thatched crotch.

"I don't want to back out."

Spur helped her lay beside him. He smothered her breasts with kisses and worked down slowly toward her pubic hair. She gasped, climaxed once quickly, then spread her legs as she realized where he was going.

"Oh, my, do you want to do that?"

"Yes," he said.

"Oh!"

He worked past her brush of blonde curls

and kissed the pinkness of her outer labia, and she boiled into a sudden and long climax that brought sweet smelling juices seeping out of her.

Bee squirmed under his ministrations.

"Lordy, I've never in my life felt anything so delicious! That was absolutely remarkable. Great!"

"Sweetheart, you haven't even started feeling good. The best is yet to come."

He thrust a finger into her vagina, and she screeched in surprise and wonder. There was no barrier there. He thrust again and reamed her, spreading her juices. Then he kissed her softly.

"Are you sure you want me to enter you, to make love with you?"

"Oh, darling yes! If you don't I'll scream and claim that you raped me."

"What choice do I have?"

Her legs parted more, he lifted her knees up and slid between them, his chest wound forgotten. She whimpered as he probed.

"Now, Bee, this may hurt a little, but it's just a stretching. Remember when you're a mother a baby's head will come out this same slot, it can stretch that large, so this is just a little bit of enlargement. It might hurt for a minute, but not much."

As he talked he probed, found the right spot and pressed harder and harder until the lubrication worked and the muscles relaxed and stretched and he slipped into her.

"Oh, Lordy! Oh, Christ! That . . . that . . . that didn't really hurt. Oh, glorious! You're inside of me! You broke through and you're fucking me!"

Spur laughed softly, then began his movements, slowly, letting her get the whole effect. She began to hum a soft little tune as her own hips began to work against his.

"Isn't it amazing that nobody has to teach a couple how to make love?" Spur said. "It's one of the few basic instincts left in man."

She didn't reply, just lay there smiling, her eyes closed, humming a little tune and working her hips against him.

Spur was in no hurry. "Do you like that?"

"Oh, Lordy, yes! I could lay here all day. Can I lift my legs?"

"Yes, it will feel different."

She put her legs up and locked them over his back, and she moaned as his erection probed a different track, touched new nerve endings and penetrated deeper.

"Oh, Lordy but that is delicious!"

Suddenly she climaxed. It was more intense this time, a rolling, surging kind that made her moan and yelp and left her so limp she couldn't say a word.

Spur waited for her, not moving for a few minutes. She roused and smiled at him.

"So wonderful! Is that what I've been telling boys I didn't want to do for the past four years? What a ninny! It is so glorious, so marvelous. I could lay here for a year!"

"It's also dangerous. Every exposure means you could get pregnant. And then the fun is over and the work begins. It means for every bit of joy and glory, there is some pain and some work ahead."

"Not if I don't get pregnant. I can watch my bleeding and only make love the day after I finish."

"Your father wants you to get married."

"Enough time for that, or when I find the right man. Oh, you're still hard inside me. You didn't yet?"

"No."

"Billy aways shot that white stuff out whenever I touched him. Sometimes he would do it three times."

"Once will be enough for me in my weakened condition."

He began to move again, and this time he punched hard and fast and left her panting. He knew she was building again, and before he climaxed she came again, the rolling, yelping, and moaning kind. He kept pounding at her, lifting her legs to his shoulders and thrusting as deep as he could reach with every stroke until he felt the flood gates open and the rush began that brought a groan from him, a surge of delight and excitement as he climaxed and panted. She had finished as well and he slumped on her. Her arms came around him when she lowered her legs, and they lay there panting, trying to recover.

"Darling do it again," she said.

He shook his head. "I couldn't for half hour, and I shouldn't. My chest is aching again. What did you tell your father about coming into town?"

"To see Betty, my friend. I come in once a week, and we talk and sew and gossip. She'll say I was there all day. I'll stop by before I go back home." She kissed him tenderly. "Once more?"

"I better not."

"You could kiss me again."

He did, a long, leisurely, exploratory kiss with mouths open and temperatures rising. He broke it off.

"You're trying to get me excited again."

"That certainly got me excited!" She rubbed her breasts against his bare chest below the bandage, then wiggled until he turned over on his back and she lowered one, then the other breast into his mouth for chewing.

"Delightful! When can we do this again?"

"Next month after your bleeding."

She laughed. "And you will be gone by next month. Daddy said you wouldn't be here long. Unless you want to stay and marry me. Then we wouldn't have to worry."

"Tempting, but I'm not ready to settle down yet either."

"But you never will get pregnant and have to."

"Hopefully."

They both laughed.

He pushed her up, felt a twinge in his chest and sat up and began dressing. She sat there naked, her blonde hair falling down her chest, covering her breasts. She stroked her hair.

"You sure about not wanting to get married? It would really please me. And you would be getting a fantastic ranch to help run, and take over when Pa can't do it anymore. A nice little dowry I'm offering."

He bent and kissed her lips, then each pointed breast.

"You make a remarkably tempting offer, even without the ranch. But I have a job to do. I travel all over the western states and territories. To California and to Washington state. What would you do sitting home alone?"

"I thought . . ."

"I know. Sex can't do it all. People participate in sex maybe three hours a week, young married people say. Three hours out of 168 a week, that's less than two percent of your time is spent getting sexy. There has to be a lot more."

He bent and petted her breasts and she reached up for a quick kiss.

"Now you better get dressed and then you can go have lunch with Betty, and tell her about your first time getting fucked."

Bee laughed. "I can't say that word unless I'm feeling real sexy." She paused for a moment, then picked up her clothes and dressed. Spur watched and she didn't mind. When she was ready for the street, Spur checked the hall, then kissed her nose and let her out.

"Maybe I can see you again," she said as she went out the door, then she walked into the hall and toward the stairs.

Spur closed the door, took a deep breath and felt his chest respond. The morning hadn't set back his recovery too much.

He would have a quick dinner in the dining room, and then see if Tyler Udell had dried out Snuffy enough to get him to talk. One witness was fine, but if they had two who could place Cain just coming into town after the massacre, they would be a lot more sure of a conviction.

# Chapter Fifteen

Spur found Tyler Udell and Snuffy in a room at the hotel and saw that Snuffy was sober enough to talk. The problem was would he remember what happened that day over a week ago.

Spur used the "cold shower" technique of questioning, pouncing on the subject and whipsawing him before he knew what happened so he had to rely on instinct and recall.

When Snuffy looked up at Spur he saw cold green eyes you could strike a match on and a steel-hard angry face.

"Snuffy, you asshole! I need to know where you were the day that stage massacre took place. I need to know right now!"

Snuffy shrank back on the bed and pulled a blanket up to his chin.

"Christ! Let me think. Yeah, that was the same day I walked out that horse. Kept the nag from foundering. And the bastard that owned her never even came back for her. Don't know where he got to. Thought for sure he'd give me a dollar for saving his horse. Christ, I learned me a lesson there."

"Shut up, Snuffy! Just answer the damn

questions. I don't need a whole long story about it! Now, who owned the horse? Who rode that nag until he almost killed her?"

"Hell, easy. Cain Haworth."

"What time of day was it?"

Snuffy laughed. "Don't got no Waterbury. Don't hold much to keeping time, 'cepting when it gets dark and light. Good enough for me."

Spur cuffed him along the side of the head and Snuffy sat up on the bed, eyes angry.

"I didn't sober you up to find out about your philosophy of life, asshole! What time was it? Morning, afternoon, dusk?"

Snuffy took a deep breath, winced and held his side, then nodded. "Yeah, all right. It was after dinner time 'cause I got thrown out of a saloon 'cause they were serving noon meal at some tables. Must have been two, three hours after that. I'd say had to be three o'clock."

Spur's attitude changed. He reached down and shook Snuffy's hand. "We might need you to testify in court about that. Can you do that? We'll give you enough notice to get sober, and get a shave and a bath. Could you stand that?"

Snuffy drew back. "You ain't gonna pop me again?"

"Nope."

"Good. Ty said might be a half a pint in it for me if I remembered what happened that day."

"True. You tell Barry over at the Petticoat that you have a tab. You get a pint a day on me for the next two weeks." Spur flipped a twenty dollar gold piece in the air and caught it. "Or would you rather have this twenty?"

Snuffy reached for it, then shook his head. "Nope. I been a drunk too long. I'd buy three pints and get skunk-drunk and somebody would steal the rest of that twenty. I'll take the pint a day."

"And get a bath, a shave and a haircut and a clean pair of pants and shirt. Otherwise Barry won't give you a pint. Ty will help you." Spur handed Ty a five dollar gold piece. He went to the door and waved, then walked out the door and headed to the Petticoat to give Barry the word.

He was back in the street when a rider came in at a gallop.

"The Santiam's dried up! Not a drop coming through her! Dry as a sandbox in August!"

Spur went to the livery barn and got a horse. He took a rifle and his six-gun and rode out of town a half mile to where the Santiam curled past.

She was bleached bone dry.

He swore softly and turned upstream. It had to be that sluice gate he had seen. Nothing else would cut the flow to nothing. What little water got under the sluice gate would vanish into the river bed long before it got to town. He rode to the Young place and found the rancher gone. His wife said six men had ridden up that morning and talked, and her husband got his rifle and two boxes of rounds for it and ridden north with the men. She wasn't sure, but she thought she recognized Mr. Longley with them.

Spur thanked her and rode up the dry river on the trail north. He hoped he wasn't too late to prevent this from blowing up into a water rights range war.

He was.

Spur heard the rifle shots while he was still a mile away from the sluice gate. Two shots sounded and a seven or eight shot burst replied. Then sporadic fire came as he rode faster.

He stopped on a small rise where he could see both sides of the stream ahead. The sluice gate had been dropped. He could see water above it, and almost none below.

Puffs of smoke showed on the rise behind the gate on the Box H land, showing where the riflemen were. On the other side of the stream there was a heavily timbered hill where the firing sounds came from. The brush and woods were too thick to spot individual blue smoke from the black powder in the rounds.

For a moment it felt as if he were back in the infantry with a blue uniform on evaluating a Rebel strongpoint. The situation was clear. Nobody was going to win. From what he could see the Haworth men had dug in, with a breastwork of logs that had firing slots cut out of them. They could hold off a company from the front.

The attackers lay just behind a stretch of nearly a hundred yards that was open land, with no cover of any kind. They would be picked off like ducks in a rain barrel if they tried an assault.

Spur turned his mount and rode at right angles to the river to the open range side, heading for the woods and the finger ridge where the attackers must be. He came down the slope quietly, heard the firings and one or two whining incoming slugs, before he tied his horse and moved cautiously toward the combatants.

McCoy had no idea what he was going to do. Stop the attack was first, but beyond that, he didn't know. If no one had been killed yet, he had a chance.

He saw the first man behind a large Douglas fir. Closer to the front of the woods nestled under Engelmann spruce were two more men. Behind an old fallen log he saw the white-haired Efrem Longley. Spur worked his way down silently toward the first man and called to him sharply from behind.

"Don't turn around, you're covered. I'm friendly, I want to talk to Longley."

The man started to turn, then nodded. "Yeah. Fine. Sounds like that federal guy. Come on past." He called ahead so the others would know Spur was coming in and Longley sat down behind the log.

"What you doing up here?"

"Trying to keep your wife from being a widow. What the hell you trying to do, get this whole county into a range war?"

"Better war than to see my cattle all die of thirst."

"We can work out something better. Any of your people been hit yet?"

"No."

"Then tell them to stop shooting and let me talk to the men across the river."

"Can't do that. We have four ranches represented here."

"Then take a vote. Somebody gets killed out here, I can guarantee you that whoever pulled the trigger is going to hang. Now is this important enough to eget killed over?"

Longley sighed. His years were slowing him down and he hated it. "We're right, McCoy. You know that we're right."

"A lot of folks who were right also are dead. You want to be one of them then you jump out of the woods and storm across that hundred yards of open space and find out for yourself."

"Nobody is going to charge them. Just want them to know we're here. We got a plan."

"I bet." Spur looked at the river from over the log. The firing had died out as the others on this side watched Longley, who was clearly their leader. Spur could see the river and the way it surged against the gate. Some flotsam had built up there already. As he watched he noticed something floating down the now sluggish current. He stared at it closer. It was a wooden box lashed to two short logs.

The shape of the box looked familiar, and then he remembered where he had seen boxes like that before.

Dynamite!

The box would hold fifty to a hundred sticks, he couldn't remember which. More than enough to blow the gate into kindling. They would let it float down to the sluice gate where it would catch against it in the jam of small brush and limbs, and then one of the men on this side would shoot into the box until the dynamite exploded.

The new gelatin explosive wasn't as stable as black powder. Even a pistol bullet would set off a stick of it.

"Don't do it, Longley."

"Do what?"

"The box of dynamite."

"Too late now, but nice try."

As they talked the current quickened and the box lodged against the gate, caught there in the limbs and trash. At once six rifles fired at the container. Spur saw the slugs slam into the gate, into the logs holding the box afloat.

Maybe the dynamite was too stable to explode.

"Tell them to stop, Longley!"

Just as the rancher stopped shooting and looked at Spur, the river in front of them erupted in a gigantic fountain as the fifty sticks of dynamite exploded in an ear shattering, crunching roar.

The wooden sluice gate dam splintered and rose in great chunks hurtling into the sky downstream. Water geysered a hundred feet in the air and mud and rocks began coming down on both sides of the river as the explosion propelled them in all directions with equal force.

A great blue cloud of smoke hung over the area for a moment, then a slapping wave of sound and rushing air slammed into the trees and whistled around them until it played out on the slopes behind.

Now all was quiet. The gate and the posts were gone. The stream lay as it had been with the exception of a ten foot deep hole in the riverbed which rapidly filled with water from upstream. It overflowed and the water swept on down the main flood plain of the river's normal course. Even the ditch that had channeled water to the Haworth lake was covered and filled by the dirt and rocks from the explosion.

In a matter of five seconds the problem had been solved and as far as Spur knew nobody wounded. But the problem wasn't solved. Only the immediate flashpoint cause had been put out of business.

Suddenly the firing from across the stream began again, and the men ducked behind trees and logs.

"Bastards!" someone shouted from the other side. "I'll kill you all for that!"

"Sounds like Cain Haworth himself," Longley said. "He never was one with a slow temper."

"If anybody comes storming across that open spot, I don't want anyone to shoot them!" Spur said during a lull in the firing from across the way. "If they come, we shoot over their heads to turn them back."

As he said it three men jumped from the brush and waded the stream.

"Wait until they get fifty yards from the trees, then on my signal, everyone fire, BUT OVER THEIR HEADS. Anyone gets killed out there, somebody in here hangs!"

Spur waited. When the three men were at the point he had selected he shouted, "Fire!"

Thirty rounds whistled and snapped over the three men's heads in the open. One turned at once and ran back to the stream. A second soon followed. The third shook his fist at the woods, fired his rifle three times, then turned and ran back to the brush on the far side of the stream.

The Longley team lay in the grass for an hour waiting. There was no response from across the way.

"I think they have given up the fight," Spur said. "Now is the time you soldiers go home, and Longley and I go pay a social call on Henry Haworth."

Two of the other ranchers grumbled, but at last nodded and found their horses deeper in the woods and rode out. Longley watched Spur and nodded.

"Damn but you would make me a good son-in-law. Sure you don't cotton to one of my daughters?"

Spur swung up into his saddle and nodded. "Matter of fact, Longley, I cotton to all three of them. Three fine ladies. One of them is going to be a school marm, I hope. The oldest one is sassy and nice and the youngest is the beauty. But I'm not a good marriage risk. I'll be gone in a week. Now, let's swing south and come up the regular trail into the Box H ranch."

"Are you going to arrest him?" Longley said after they had the ranch in sight.

"Why?"

"He has violated our water rights."

"True. But what if he didn't order the sluice gate closed?"

"Who, then?"

"We'll have to wait and see."

Spur knew there had to be a confrontation with Haworth. It had to come now, but he had no idea of the outcome. This would make three felonies he could charge Haworth with if he had ordered the water diverted. He also had to pick up Cain Haworth and charge him with the killings.

The sentry at the first gate frowned when he saw them.

"Mr. Haworth told me not to let anyone past," the cowhand said. The rifle was held loosely in his hands pointing at the ground.

Spur's six-gun came up quickly, covering the man.

"Doesn't matter, this is official law enforcement business. If you have any objection to that you ride ahead of us with both hands on the saddle horn."

"You that federal lawman?" the guard asked.

"That's right, Spur McCoy, United States Secret Service."

"That's good enough for me. I'll tell them that someone is coming."

He started to lift the rifle.

"No," Spur said. He motioned for Longley to ride near the man and take the rifle and his pistol. "Let's ride up and see the man of the house."

Henry Haworth was on the front porch waiting for them when they rode in. From the looks of his face, Spur figured that he knew about the sluice gate, the dynamite, and the small war. His face was haggard, his eyes sunken and red. His scraggly sparse hair in disarray. Haworth leaned heavily on a gold headed cane.

"Reckon you know about the river."

"Yes. Did you order the gate closed?"

"No."

"Who did?"

"Cain. He took four men and went out just before dark last night. Didn't tell me. We still got plenty of water. It was a mistake that you corrected."

"Where is your son, Cain, Mr. Haworth?"

"Left. Soon as the explosion happened, he rode home fast and charged out of here with two horses. He headed for town."

"You mind if we confirm that with some of your hands?"

"No. Anything else?"

Spur saw that the old rancher was about to collapse. Lot came out and put his arm around his father, supporting him. Lot looked at Spur and nodded.

"I saw Cain ride out, Mr. McCoy. He had two rifles with him, and lots of ammunition. He took his two hand guns too. Said Darlow and Olsen were not going to get him in trouble. What did he mean by that?"

"We'll have to find out, Lot. If you say Cain left, I'll take your word for it. Thanks for the help of the Box H crew for the work on the two houses."

Lot nodded. "Least we can do. The barns will be next, the middle of August. We'll get it planned ahead of time."

Spur tipped his hat and walked with Longley back toward where the horses were tied at the rail. Longley gave the guard his weapons, and the two men mounted and rode toward town.

"So Cain is running," Longley said. "It doesn't seem reasonable for him to light out because of the sluice gate thing."

"He's running from more that that. He's the one who killed those six people on that stage."

Longley sighed. "It figures. Never have had much use for the boy. And he's been trying to come courting Bee for three or four months now. She told me not to let him."

Spur reset his low crowned gray hat. "I think we better move along a little faster. I got me a bad feeling about this Cain Haworth."

# Chapter Sixteen

As soon as the two riders came into town Spur knew there was trouble. Groups of men and women talked on street corners. There was a knot of men around the sheriff's office. People in the street seemed to be waiting for something. Spur and Longley rode to the little court house and tied up their horses.

"It's her father!" somebody in the crowd said.

Mrs. Longley came bursting from the group of people near the sheriff's office and threw herself into her husband's arms. She was sobbing. He looked at her curiously, patting her back and talking quietly. Then he listened carefully to what she told him.

"Efrem, somebody took Bee! He stopped our buggy and looked at us and then told Bee to get out. It was awful. He had his guns!" She shivered and sobbed against his shoulder. Then went on.

"Bee wouldn't get down from our buggy. The man on the horse with the gun was Cain Haworth, and she's told me several times that he has bothered her and she doesn't like him. Then he rode up and grabbed her and pulled her onto his horse. I screamed at him and hit him with the buggy whip. He fired two shots over my head and then rode out of town to the east."

Longley headed for the sheriff's office. Quigley met them at the boardwalk.

"It was Cain Haworth," Quigley said. "We have two witnesses who identified him. Our posse is almost ready and we'd like you to come."

"I want to go along, too," Spur said. The sheriff nodded.

It was almost three o'clock that afternoon before they knew for sure where Cain and his heavily loaded horse were headed. He had started east, then circled around to the south and was on a honey-bee streak for the Longley ranch. The posse rode faster then, not bothering to track more than every half mile or so.

The group consisted of two deputies, and three townsmen who were reliable, sturdy and good shots. The sheriff had recruited them as special posse members for emergencies. This was no rag tag mob out for blood. Rather it was a trained unit, used to working together and all willing to obey the sheriff's orders.

"He's gonna burn down my buildings," Efrem Longley said as he charged along at the head of the posse.

Spur figured Cain was looking for a pair of

fresh horses. He would know he couldn't stay ahead of a mounted posse for long double loaded. There would be little time for anything other than saddling new mounts and making sure the girl didn't run away.

When they came within sight of the Longley ranchhouse, they saw it was still standing. Nothing had been burned. Both girls and three of the hands were in the front yard. The hands had been tied to a tree and were still trying to get lose. The girls were solemn and Mary had red eyes from crying.

Delilah told them what happened.

"This man came riding up with Bee, shot at one of our hands and made him tie up the other two, then dragged Bee to the barn and pretty soon they rode out the side door, both on fresh horses. They went south."

"Did he hurt you?" Longley demanded. Both girls shook their heads. Longley ran inside and came back with two boxes of shells for his rifle and headed south. The posse followed.

A half mile below the buildings, Cain evidently had ridden into the shallows of the Santiam. The group had to split, working both sides of the river to find out where he came out. At the current low level of the river, he could ride along it for miles and leave no prints.

That's what he did. The sun was staring to go down and still the posse was split across the river.

"He'll come out sooner or later," Sheriff Quigley said. "He can't camp overnight in the water."

An hour later it was dark and they still had not found the tracks leaving the water.

Spur had been holding his side as he rode. It hurt, but not enough to make him stay behind. He studied the river and the gently rolling plain. Cain was no more than an hour ahead of them. How had he stayed out of sight? Now he could leave the water and ride all night. He could walk the horses and still cover four miles an hour. From dawn to dusk he could put forty miles between him and the searchers.

Quigley looked at his seven men. "Can't do much until it gets light," he said.

Spur shook his head. "He wants us to stop, Sheriff. Put yourself in his shoes, what would you do?"

"I don't know."

Longley spoke up. "What I would do is slow us down, like he did with the ride in the water, then when the sun went down, I'd get back on land and move as fast as I could for as long as the horses would hold out, then find some thick brush and hide."

"That's good, Longley," Spur said. About the way I'd play it, Sheriff, this is your command, but could I make a suggestion?"

"Yes."

"Let me take Longley and two men and move out along the river. We probably won't

186

find any tracks, but odds are he will move on down the river route because it's flat and easy going beside it. What we might find is a campfire, or hear some sound. Anything is better than all of us sitting here. We will have you and your men here as a background in case he tries to double back."

"You find anything fire three shots and we'll catch up," the sheriff said.

Spur nodded and Longley took one of the men the sheriff designated and moved across the hock deep water. Spur and the other deputy moved down this side of the stream. They agreed to keep in contact with each other by lighting a match every mile or so.

Spur gave up trying to read the ground for any sign. Even with the partly cloudly moonlight, it was impossible. They would move slowly, watching for fircs and listening. Spur hoped he wouldn't hear any screams.

Spur figured by the location of the big dipper that it was nearly midnight. He had just seen the flare of a match across the stream, and gave an answering one. When he looked south again he saw a glow in the sky. Fire!

"Longley!" Spur shouted. "See that fire ahead? Is there a ranch down that way?"

"Yeah, Iverson. He's on your side of the river. We better ride!"

By the time they covered the two miles to the Iverson ranch, the barn was burned down. Iverson sat on the steps of his house watching. He had a bullet in his shoulder.

"Damn Cain Haworth!" he told them. "Pranced in here and demanded two fresh horses. I said no. He shot me. No warning, just blew me into the ground. Then he took two horses, changed the saddles, took your daughter, Longley, and rode out south."

"How was Bee? Had he hurt her? Was he forcing her to go along with him?"

"Damn right he was forcing her. She tried to talk to me and he told her to shut up. He almost hit her. That kid had a wild look in his eye."

"She was . . . was still dressed proper?"

"Yes. I don't think he'd had time to do anything. Efrem, I'd like to ride with you, but I couldn't help much."

"You stay put, Bill," Longley said. "Come daylight you get into town and have Doc Varner look at that shoulder. We better be moving on."

"How long ago did they leave, Mr. Iverson?" Spur asked.

"Not more than an hour, maybe less. Good luck."

"We'll leave these two men here in case he comes back and tries to burn your house. The deputies will signal the sheriff to come down and wait with you. We'll move out and try to trail Cain. You tell the sheriff what happened when he comes."

They rode.

The best route south was along a county

road that passed near the ranch house and wound to south and east, away from the river. Spur rode for a quarter of a mile, then stopped, lit a stinker match and a handful of dead grass and checked the dusty roadway. There were tracks of two horses, both moving fast. There were no night insect tracks over the hoof prints as there were on those made earlier in the day. These were the right tracks.

They rode for another hour. The moon came out brightly. Every half mile they stopped and checked the trail, which had turned into something of a wagon road. The same pair of prints were there.

Spur felt they were gaining on the killer. He had no good evidence, he simply sensed it. They came to a spot of woods near a feeder stream where the trail forded across under an archway of a dark tunnel. Spur slowed. It looked dangerous.

The pair of rifle shots came like a booming death knell in the dark silence of the Montana night. Spur bent low on the far side of his horse. He heard a cry and saw Longley slump in the saddle and bring his mount to a stop.

Spur tugged at the reins and brought his mount around to grab Longley's horse. He led it to the side of the trail and dismounted on the wrong side catching Efrem as he tumbled from the saddle.

"Where are you hit?"

"Thigh. Hurts like hell. Think it broke my leg."

Spur helped him die down in the grass. Another rifle round slammed over their heads. It came from across the trail and twenty yards down.

Longley nodded and bent to bind up his leg.

Spur darted across the road, running low and hard. The hidden rifle spoke again, but the lead missed. McCoy slid into the brush quietly, not making a sound and listened. If Cain was the gunman, Bee had to be there too. He listened. At first he could only hear the crickets and a night hawk. It was probably a North American goatsucker. An owl hooted down the trail.

Then he heard movement. Man movement. A twig cracked, leaves rustled. To the left and going away from him. Spur knew he couldn't fire while the girl was with Cain. He moved in the direction of the pair, testing each step, careful not to make a sound.

After ten steps he paused. The sounds came from ahead of him, but closer.

A horse nickered somewhere beyond.

Someone yelped in pain.

Whispers followed, all ahead.

Spur moved faster, testing steps, checking as far as he could see in the darkness of the brushy area.

"No!" a woman's voice said indignantly.

A hand hit flesh with a slapping sound.

Spur rushed forward, his pistol out, his

face a mask of anger. Suddenly he broke out of the woods. Ahead two dark shapes showed in the moonlight as horses. He fired his pistol into the air and dove to one side.

"No, no! I won't. Help me whoever you are!"

Spur fired again, over the heads of the horses.

There was a scream. Then a man cursed, and Spur heard saddle leather creaking. Spur leaped up and charged toward the first horse. The one behind it wheeled away and rode.

"He's getting away!" Bee Longley shouted.

Spur was sure then, he emptied his six-gun at the fading black blob in the dark night, then called softly.

"Bee, where are you?"

"Over here. He tied me to some bush."

Spur found her, cut the rope and told her where her father was and that he was wounded.

"Go through the woods here and call to him. Help tie up his leg. You could get a fire going too, after I'm gone. I'll take your horse, it's fresher than mine."

She clung to him, then reached up and kissed him. "Good luck, wonderful man," she said.

Spur stepped into the saddle and swung the horse down the trail south. Now the fugitive had less of a head start, and he had lost his trump card. Now they would play the game according to Spur's rules, which meant there were no rules, it was kill or be killed.

Spur began by riding down the road at full gallop for a quarter of a mile. Then he took the Spencer and fired seven shots down the road and at slight angles to it. Spur pulled off the road into a patch of woods and wiped down his horse, staked it out where it could graze and lay down with his head against a tree trunk and his right hand closed around his six-gun.

Spur was aching tired. His side hurt again. He needed some rest. He had been up for almost twenty hours. As he thought about Cain, he decided this was the second night Cain had not had any sleep. The night before he had been closing down the sluice gate, and tonight he was running. A few rifle rounds over his head would convince him he had to keep right on running. Spur would be up at the first signs of light and start tracking him. He should have three hours of sleep.

Morning came slowly. The sun was hidden by a light overcast, and as Spur jumped up and checked his weapons, he was afraid that it might rain and wash out Cain's tracks. On the other hand the land needed a good soaking.

He was in the saddle a few moments later, checked the road and found the hoofprints that showed no oddity, and worked down the road. He rode in hundred yard spurts, then paused and studied the ground from the back of the roan he had borrowed from Bee. Cain's trail was still straight down the road, and the marks showed that he was pushing the horse. If he foundered on him out here he would be in deep trouble.

Two miles farther along the wagon road, Spur noticed that the horseshoe prints were lighter now, without so much toe thrown dirt. The mount had slowed almost to a walk.

The next time he checked the horse was wandering from side to side on the road, as though either the rider was sleeping, or the horse was in the first stages of giving out.

Spur came to a small rise and studied the land ahead of him. The light overcast had burned off and the sun shone brightly again. There would be no rain today. He could see five miles south, half that to the east and west. No smoke showed. He saw no ranches or houses. Nor could he see Cain ahead on the straight road.

He rode half a mile this time before he checked the tracks. They were more erratic than before. It was the horse now, Spur had seen the signs many times before. There were uneven hoof marks, side to side motion, and here and there dark streaks on the dirt that could only be unintentional urination.

He walked his mount now, watching the trail carefully. On a hunch he moved off the road, angled a quarter of a mile into the plains and rode hard south again just out of sight of the trail, then worked back to the road through a copse of brush and small willow and cottonwood trees. Nobody near the roadway could see him come.

On this new stretch of roadway, he could find no evidence that Cain's horse had passed over this section. Spur tied his mount in some brush and worked through fringes of high grass and trees north near the edge of the trail.

Ahead lay more of the light brush. A short distance beyond lay a swale with the dry course of a creek surrounded by dozens of small trees. There were no evergreens.

Spur remembered when he had burned out one killer with a grass fire, but that wouldn't work here. He squirmed forward through the grass and shrubs, working toward the heaviest part of the hardwood trees. He found a fist-sized rock and threw it thirty yards in the brush. The stone hit a tree bounced off through dry leaves and cracked when it hit another rock on the ground.

Twin shots thundered into the spot from somewhere to the left. Spur watched but saw only tendrils of blue smoke drifting up through the thick growth.

He angled toward the smoke, moving as cautiously and quietly as he could. Cain must be awake, or partly awake to hear the rock hit. But after being without any real sleep for going on fifty-two hours, he also must be bleary eyed, jumpy, his nerves raw bands stretched drum tight.

Spur worked through the grass and light brush on his belly, pulling the Spencer with him, holding his Eagle Butt Peacemaker in his right fist.

He worked another six feet forward and a ruffled grouse took off a foot ahead of him in a wing flapping thunder that sounded twice as loud because of the surprise. Spur rolled four feet to his right just as two slugs zipped through the grass where he had been. Grouse don't panic unless someone is right on top of them, and Cain would know that.

Spur waited for five minutes, listening, watching. He heard nothing. Perhaps his quarry was sleeping.

He worked forward again, came to an open place and stared out from behind a heavily leafed shrub. Under a large cottonwood tree he saw a black hulk. A horse was tied deeper in the shadows. As his eyes probed the hulk again, he realized it was a lean-to of sorts. Boards had been pushed against the trunk of the tree forming a dark cave.

Spur couldn't see inside it. As he looked past the lean-to he decided that if Cain had been here, he had a clear view of the trail less than twenty yards away. An easy bushwhacking murder.

Nothing moved in the dimness of the lean-to. Spur put three slugs through the opening and rolled to his left. There was no response.

He fired again, and rushed the small shelter. Just as he came up to it he smelled the smoke, then heard the sputtering of a fuse.

Dynamite fuse!

He leaped away from the opening, trying to shield himself behind the thick tree trunk.

The explosion thundered through the morning light, splattering the boards of the shelter backwards in a froth of splinters and dirt, sending a cloud of smoke into the sky, and blinding Spur with dust from the explosion.

Spur rolled, feeling the pain in his chest from the old wound, then came up with his pistol cocked and ready. From across the clearing a rifle barked and a round dug into the ground an inch from Spur's knee. He realized that was all of him the shooter could see around the tree.

McCoy stood up quickly for total protection behind the cottonwood, and looked behind him. He had no other cover to run to. He was cut off, and the man ahead of him carried a rifle.

# Chapter Seventeen

Spur bent low and peered quickly around the base of the big tree at knee height. He saw only a rifle poked over the lip of the small creek where it had cut deeply into the soil. The rifle spoke and a round thudded into the big tree.

After drawing back for a moment Spur reached around tree and put a round into the dirt directly beside the rifle barrel. He couldn't rush forward. It was a long time until darkness. He had no dynamite bombs. He took a quick look around the other side of the tree head high. Yes, the ground slanted downward to the river. By crawling straight away from the tree, Spur would be out of the direct line of sight of Haworth. It was worth a try. He checked the angle, bellied down into the grass and crawled away from the big tree seeing that the land slanted down on this side of the tree as well. After thirty feet he got to his knees and bent over double he raced for the fringe of brush again and its protecting cover.

Once there, Spur checked his rifle, which he had been dragging behind him, and made sure it was ready to fire. Then he worked his way around to the side of the big tree, moving without sound, searching for the wanted man's horse. Or did he have a horse? Spur had thought he saw one tied in the woods, but it couldn't be in any shape to ride.

His own horse!

Spur reversed his direction and ran flat out, not worrying about the noise now. He got to a spot where he could see his horse and lay down in the brush, hidden from view and waited.

It was less than two minutes later when he saw Cain working through the woods toward the mount. Spur let him get almost to the horse, then slammed a .52 caliber round from the Spencer through Cain's right leg. He went down in a heap, spun and fired three times with his pistol.

"Give it up, Cain. Your horse is gone, you're wounded, and the posse is less than an hour behind us. You don't have a chance."

"What kind of a chance do you think I have against a jury in High Prairie?" He fired twice more, then began crawling away. A moment later he was out of sight.

Spur worked forward carefully. He had the advantage now, he didn't want to lose it. He was just beyond his horse when Cain's rifle spoke sharply. The round missed Spur by a dozen feet, but he knew he wasn't the target when the borrowed horse behind him screamed in mortal pain and went down, legs kicking in fury, the sickening scream of the dying animal coming again and again, until at last the legs were stilled and so was the death cry.

Spur worked forward again, crouching in the brush, eyeing the way ahead. What if he was wrong? If Cain's horse was still sound, the man would be gone for good.

McCoy lifted up now and ran from brush clump to clump, not knowing where Cain was, but gambling that he was well away from this part of the woods. Spur circled and found the spot where he thought he had seen the horse. It was there lying on its side. As he watched he could see no movement.

He had to know.

The Secret Service man pushed closer, then took another chance and dashed the last ten yards across open ground and touched the animal. Already it had started to stiffen. The beast had been ridden to death.

Spur ran back the way he had come, worked up to the spot where he had wounded Cain and looked for blood stains. He found them on leaves and blades of grass.

Slowly he began to track Cain Haworth. The young man was clever and knew the country. McCoy worked down the dry stream, running after rounding bends in the shallow draw when he knew he was out of sight, working more slowly when he would be in Cain's firing view.

Within half an hour the dry water course

had emptied its sand into the Santiam. Despite the low water above, this downstream section had picked up enough feeder creeks to make it a worthwhile small river again. Spur checked up and down the water, but could see no wounded man. Every few steps in the sand he had found small damp spots where a drop of blood had soaked into the dryness.

The Santiam was not deep enough to allow a man to float down it on a log yet. At least that choice was not allowed the fugitive.

Spur's nose twitched. Smoke! A light wind blew up the small valley he was in. He had seen no buildings. The smoke meant an Indian camp, a homesteader, or a traveler's campfire. He was sure that Cain had not stopped to build a fire. Cain still ran ahead of him. The droplets of blood indicated that he might be slowing down a little. As the chase slowed, and Spur relaxed somewhat, the nagging pain in his upper left chest came pounding back at him. He fought it down, deliberately thought of something else, and moved back into the brush along the creek as he went downstream.

The fugitive would be at the fire, wherever it was.

Spur found it twenty minutes later. The homesteader's cabin was minimal to meet the requirements to "improve" the one hundred and sixty acres. The owner had "cultivated" a half acre to match that need, and had built three pens out of poles for his cows. He would be a rancher, not a farmer.

He would be if he survived today.

The cabin was twenty yards beyond the stream, made of logs hauled in from the timbered slopes, chinked and mortared. A clothes line behind the cabin showed a woman's petticoats and a man's work pants and shirts. No children's clothes.

Spur knew at once that he could not show himself. With all the caution at his command, Spur moved forward in the woods, until he could see the front door of the cabin. There was also a well there, a bucket and windlass with a ratchet and a rope to reach the water.

A small barn at the far side was now only a shed, with the promise of more later. Twenty head of calves bawled in the pens, and it seemed that this rancher was just getting his start the hard way.

A pistol shot echoed through the morning air. Spur wondered if it were still morning. He hadn't thought about the time. He waited, that was all he could do now. McCoy wondered if the man of the house were dead or wounded. As he thought about it, the heavy door opened, and Cain came out with a woman held in front of him as a shield.

"Spur McCoy! I know you're out there, you bastard. I know you. You tracked me. You just caused this homesteader in here to die. It's all your fault. You want this pretty woman to die too? Answer me or I'll slit her throat right now!"

Chances are he wouldn't. The woman was his only bargaining chip, he wouldn't kill her, Spur decided.

Cain shouted at him for five minutes, holding the woman. Cain could see now that she was bare above the waist. Small breasts showed over Cain's arm that viced around her stomach.

Then Cain changed his tactics. His right hand came out with a knife, and he held the woman and made a slice across her right breast.

She screamed, a wailing protest of fear and anger and pain and suffering. Spur sighted in with the rifle. He was eighty yards away. An easy shot. But he wasn't sure if the weapon had been sighted in or not. An inch one way or the other and the wrong person could die. He looked at legs, but the woman was big enough to cover Cain completely.

Spur bit his lip and waited for the woman's screams to die out.

"It's all your fault, McCoy. She wouldn't be suffering this way if you threw out your weapons. I'll let you walk away from here free. I'll take the horse and you can go your way." He laughed when Spur didn't respond.

McCoy fired. The rifle round went precisely where Spur had aimed it, maybe a half inch to the left. Now he knew where the rifle would fire. The bullet smashed into the door jamb and splintered wood fragments into the pair but neither one was hurt.

Cain screamed at him. Spur was sure the man's eyes were wild with fear and anger, the way they had been in the saloon that night. He touched the tip sight on the end of the rifle with his wet finger, then sighted in again. This time when Cain reached around to cut the woman again, Spur aimed and fired rapidly, the slug slashing through Cain's lower arm, breaking both bones, driving him back inside the cabin. He slammed the door but for several minutes Spur could hear the man wailing in pain and anger.

As soon as the door shut Spur ran. He circled the clearing looking for horses. He found two behind the shed, which housed two milk cows. The shed could not be seen from the side window of the house. Quickly Spur put halters on the two horses and led them directly away from the shed into the woods, then ran with them a half mile down the small valley through the trees, and tied them to brush where they could graze.

By the time he got back to the cabin, it seemed to be much the way it had been before. Spur went to the side of the house with no window and ran the twenty yards to the log cabin. He pressed against the cabin, panting. As his breath came back, he fisted his six-gun and worked around to the corner, checked to be sure no one was on the other side, then edged up to the window with four, foot-square panes of glass, and peered inside.

It was a one room cabin. On the far wall he saw a small fireplace and cooking gear on the hearth. There was no stove. On the wall to the right stood a homemade bed with a mattress of straw and grass, Spur guessed. Lying face down on the blanket was a man in rough work clothes. A large red stain of blood thickened beneath his head.

Spur ducked down and went to the other side of the window to look at the other half of the house. He saw the woman had been tied to a chair. She was naked. Her legs had been spread and Cain sat in front of her laughing. Spur lifted the Peacemaker and sighted through the window. It was an angle. Would that make the bullet deflect? Probably. Cain sat with his side to Spur and his pants were around his knees. Spur aimed just below Cain's arm at his side, and fired.

The bullet hit the glass pane, and deflected enough to miss Cain, but slashed through the upper outside of the woman's thigh.

Cain reacted with the first sound of breaking glass, rolling toward the window and out of range. Three shots blasted through the other window panes, and Spur ran around the house to the door and tried to open it. Locked, or braced shut. He kicked it. It gave a little. Three more kicks with all his weight behind it and the door gave way.

Spur had reloaded as he ran, now he swung the six-gun into the house and darted inside.

Cain was gone. The wood frame of the window had been lifted out and Cain had gone through it. Spur looked out, saw a form running into the far woods. He paused only long enough to cut the woman free, told her he would be back to help her, and rushed out of the house.

Spur peered cautiously around the end of the big logs that formed the first row of the structure. Cain would be lying in wait up there, ready to pick him off with the rifle the moment he moved out across the open spot. Spur had to go the long way. He went to the front of the house, and ran directly ahead for the woods. He made it without attracting any shots. Once in the cover of the trees, he ran to the right, to circle the short side of the clearing to the point where Cain had escaped.

As he ran Spur felt his energy and his desire weakening. He was still wounded, he had been up for two days with almost no sleep, and he was so tired he could barely stand.

Then he thought of Cain. He had been up almost three days without sleep. He was wounded twice in the leg and arm, and he was the one running.

Spur snorted, made sure his weapons were both ready to fire, and hurried along the plain and easy to follow trail. Now he had to think the way the hunted man would. What would he do? What would he try?

Cain's first priority would be to kill Spur.

If not kill him, disable him. That meant a trap, an ambush. Spur knew he was in better physical condition than Cain who had a serious leg wound, a broken arm, and had to be still losing blood from it. Spur paused and listened.

They were in heavier timber again, with a few Douglas firs and Engelmann spruce dotting the hard woods. Cain could hide behind any of the big conifers and pick him off with the rifle.

Spur heard nothing. Then a scream came from somewhere ahead. Was it a trap, a trick? Had Cain simply fallen on his wounded arm, or tripped and hurt his leg? Spur had to find out. He took a calculated risk and ran up the slope to the ridgeline fifty feet above.

Spur heard the roar and looked to his right. Through the thin brush and conifers he saw a grizzly bear rear up on its hind feet and tower eight feet in the air. The beast made a swiping motion at something and a pistol fired. Just ahead of the advancing king of the northwoods, Spur saw a flash of Cain going down. He wasn't sure if the grizzly had hit Cain or if he dove to escape the mighty paw. If the swing had connected it was powerful enough to tear off an arm, or a head.

Another pistol shot fired and Spur saw now that Cain was under the bear, and five or six hundred pound beast was growling and roaring in fury. Cain edged backward, scuffling along on his hands and feet, his back to the ground, his eyes watching the animal hovering over him.

Spur made the decision without considering the circumstances. A man simply does not let a human being be mauled and devoured by a grizzly bear.

The Spencer roared three times, as fast as Spur could pull the lever to eject the spent cartridge and pump in a new one. There was no desire to kill the magnificent beast. All the shots hit the bear in the left shoulder and it roared in pain and turned toward its new enemy.

Cain jumped up and raced into the heavy timber, and Spur saw that he carried only his pistol, the rifle lost somewhere in his surprise by the grizzly.

Spur realized the big animal could run faster and farther than he could if he were unhurt. But the bear had three .52 caliber slugs in one shoulder and that would slow him down.

The Secret Service Agent charged downhill, through the light brush in the same direction Cain had gone. In a way he now regretted his humane act. The grizzly would have killed the pistol wielding puny little man. Then it would have been over. Perhaps the terror of being torn apart by a grizzly would have been a fit punishment for the crime.

Spur kept running. He could hear Cain crashing through brush ahead. There was no attempt at stealth now, only for survival, and that meant putting as much distance as physically possible between themselves and the infuriated grizzly.

The course carried Spur past the side of the low valley and up the side of a slope. He saw Cain for a moment as he vanished over the ridgeline. The fugitive was moving slower now. Spur turned and ran thirty yards parallel so he would come to the ridge in a different area.

Moving up slowly in a new position may have saved McCoy's life. He peered cautiously over the ridge, the bear forgotten now, the enemy with a deadly weapon became important again. Just across the ridge and near the point he had crossed, Cain lay beside a tree, his pistol up and ready.

Spur could see only the edge of his face and a hand with a six-gun. McCoy had no shot, not even with the rifle. Silently Spur edged back across the ridgeline and hurried ten yards toward the ambush point. When he peered over the ridge again past a heavy growth of grass, he saw that Cain had left.

Ahead Spur heard the man running again. There couldn't be much energy left in Cain. He would hole up soon. Cain was hunting a defensive position, and he knew the territory.

It was slow going for a while, as McCoy tracked the quarry running through the brushy woods. More Douglas fir showed now and Ponderosa pine and a sprinkling of

Western larch. None of the trees had been harvested, it was sparse but virgin timber land.

The trail led to a valley, and then turned up a small flowing stream a yard wide. The gurgling water became a drinking fountain for Spur who didn't realize how thirsty he was. His canteen was on his dead horse.

To Spur's surprise he saw a thin column of smoke coming from the canyon. He was sure Cain's tracks led in that direction. There could be only one reason for the smoke: it was a trap. Spur worked into heavier woods beside the stream and moved up cautiously. He had less than a hundred yards to go.

Spur's mind and every nerve ending in his body were alert to the slightest detail that might be out of place or dangerous. He saw nothing, no trip wires, no deadfalls, no snare that would lift him high in the air after catching one foot. Nothing.

Spur made the final thrust toward the smoke. He could smell it now, see tendrils lifting through the trees. Then he spotted the source. The fire had been built in the mouth of a small cave that became a dark circle in the far bank of the stream. A cave, a fortress. The perfect defensive position.

McCoy stared at the cave and knew the chase was not over.

# Chapter Eighteen

Spur lay in the woods and watched the hole. Slowly he realized it was more than a cave. It was a tunnel, a mine tunnel that must have been there for years. The remains of tailings showed on both sides of the small creek that ran down and into the Santiam.

What was left of a wagon road could be seen on the far side of the stream. Young fir and larch trees had grown up and brush covered part of the old tracks. A mine, not just a cave. That presented a whole new problem. Sometimes mines had more than one entrance.

At once he made an assumption that this one probably didn't. It would have had to be extensive and successful for that kind of a tunnel and shaft system.

Maybe Spur could wait for Cain to put more fuel on the fire and nail him with a round at the mouth of the tunnel. Just then some branches came out of the darkness and landed on the fire. It was too late to shoot by the time Spur brought up the Spencer.

A voice boomed from the cave, distorted and faint, but Spur could hear it.

"McCoy. You must be out there by now. You've had an hour to find the smoke. Come on and get me, bastard! Come and find me. I used to work in this mine. I know every square foot of it and I can run you around for months in here."

Spur did not respond. Cain wouldn't know if he were outside the tunnel mouth yet or not. When the monologue finished, Spur moved slowly, working closer to the cave. He crossed the stream and ran toward the tunnel. The agent was well to one side and out of sight. If Cain came close enough to call out again, Spur would act.

Time didn't matter now. It was permanently midnight in the mine. There must be some torches. Enough of that for later. He hoped he could finish the chase near the entrance.

It was almost an hour later when Spur heard movement inside the tunnel. Spur had worked up soundlessly until he now stood just outside the square set framing of the tunnel mouth. The agent could hear the footsteps, saw sparks fly as the unseen man tossed wood on the fire, then the voice came.

"McCoy, you might as well come get me, I'm never going . . ."

The rest of the words were blasted by sound as Spur leaped in front of the tunnel and fired six times with his six-gun and then jumped back. He pushed the rifle around the timbers and fired five more times into the

211

hole.

When the echoes of the barrage faded into the distance, Spur heard a sullen laugh.

"Close, but no prize, lawman. A good tactic, but not good enough. Now come and get me!"

Spur pushed the spent rounds from his pistol and pushed new ones in. He checked his pockets. He had fresh packets of stinkers, the cardboard matchsticks with sulphur and salt peter on the ends that could be struck on the bottom and lighted. He reloaded the Spencer so it had seven rounds in the tubular magazine that slid in through the stock. The Spencer 1860 7-shot repeating rifle had half the range of the new army Springfield .45 caliber rifle. But he preferred it for short work.

His ears had been straining, but he had heard nothing from the tunnel. There had been no shots. Perhaps Cain was getting short on rounds for his pistol. Perhaps he was out of ammunition.

Spur knew he would backlight himself the moment he started into the tunnel. He would do it quickly, from this side of the front of the tunnel to the far side just inside. A running, diving roll would do it. He pressed at the bandage high on his chest and hoped it would hold for one more diving roll.

He waited another five minutes, then turned, ran forward, dove at the front of the timbers and rolled inside, coming to his feet and pressing against the rough rock wall.

There had been no shots, no attack. He let his eyes widen to accustom himself to the dim light. Torches, there should be some close at hand. Or had they all been used up by wandering explorers?

He stared hard at the walls near the front and found a torch. It was a two foot fir branch. The end had been injured when still on the tree and it grew a thick pad of "pitch" around the wound. The pitch was solid turpentine, and burned with a brilliant flame. Pitch sticks would start on fire even when soaking wet because the water could not penetrate the cells of the heavy pitch wood.

Spur carried the stick, slung the rifle over his back on the strap, and put the Peacemaker in his right hand. He moved forward slowly.

There had not been rails in the tunnel, or if there had they were gone now. The dirt floor was cluttered with fallen rocks and dirt and stones from the ceiling and walls. Here there was no framing, just a naked tunnel cut through the rock and earth. The rock had been firm enough to hold the ceiling. The tunnel was seven feet high and most of the opening was six feet wide.

Spur walked softly for twenty feet and realized that he could see no more than two or three feet in front of him, and that distance was becoming shorter. He had to use the torch, and maybe become a target, or he had to turn around.

He knelt down and took out the stinkers. Hope more than logic told him that Cain was down to his last three or four shots in the pistol. He would use them carefully, use them to kill, not on a wild long shot.

Spur struck match to the fir pitch and saw it catch at once. He couldn't have had a better torch if he had soaked a gunny sack in coal oil and wired it to a stick.

The pitch blazed up brighter and brighter, and Spur held the branch at arm's distance in front of him and hurried along the tunnel.

Twenty feet farther in he came to a drift, a side tunnel that hd been cut in exploring for, or removing, ore. He checked it and found it was only a dozen feet deep, but it had been dug out fifteen feet high. There was a long iron rod with a sharp point on one end that had been dulled, and a round ball on the other that had been slammed repeatedly with a sledge. It was a slow, cheap kind of hand drill, that would be held by one man, pounded by another, and turned with every blow.

Spur went back to the main tunnel and listened.

Nothing.

He worked down the path faster now, cleared three more drifts to each side and came soon to a wider, higher place where timbers were positioned in the center and bolted in place. When he looked closer with the torch he saw it was a shaft that went straight down. Spur dropped a rock down and listened for it to hit the bottom. It went down a long way before he heard the sound of bottom. There was a tattered remains of a two-inch rope hanging six feet into the shaft.

Cain wasn't down there, unless he was dead at the bottom.

Spur moved around the vault-like room and found four more tunnels leading off. He guessed now that this must have been a producing mine of some sort, that had been long abandoned.

He looked up when he heard the sound. The light from the torch did not carry far enough for him to find the source. It seemed to be coming from one of the tunnels that went out like spokes. Then he saw the rails on the center tunnel and he jumped off the thin steel rails that extended into the darkness.

A moment later an ore car eight feet long and weighing hundreds of pounds thundered down the rails and slammed into the foot thick timbers at the dump point. When the sound faded, Spur heard laughter up the track.

Now he had a direction.

The pine knot burned brightly, but he caught another one and carried it with him. There were more of the torches up this way. Here there was evidence that the mine had been worked more recently. Piles of ore showed on the floor at the end of some of the drifts. He found a shovel and a pick in one of the drifts where they had been left by some weary miner.

The ceiling of the main tunnel was lower here. In some spots Spur had to bend over to get under. Here and there he saw square sets of timbers that roofed up what must be soft spots in the ceiling.

Once when he looked ahead into the darkness he saw the glimmer of a torch. He fired at it, only to have his eardrums assaulted by the thunderous explosion of the .45 in the confined space of the tunnel, where the sound slammed from one close wall to the other, and reverberated through the whole mine, the vibrations causing sifts of sand and dirt to pour down from the ceiling, and in some cases small rockfalls came down.

He moved ahead faster now, not checking the side drifts until he came to the point where he figured the torch had been.

He saw the light well before he got there. It was another "room" dug out where they must have found a large deposit of ore. The area was twenty feet high and twice that wide. Six torches had been lighted and put in holders around the walls. The black oily smoke lifted to the roof where it hung in blue waves.

Spur saw at once that four more tunnels led out of the room. He marked the one he left by knocking a pair of fresh chips off the blue-gray rock by the entrance. Spur could see no one in the enclosure. Cain had to be in one of the other tunnels, waiting for an easy shot.

"You might as well surrender, Cain. You have nowhere to go. This is the end of the line. We can starve you out if nothing else. We don't have to wade in there and trade .45 rounds with you. You're a dead man if you stay here. You have a chance with a judge and a jury."

"No chance at all, you know that!" Cain shot back at him. The voice was high, strange, wild.

"Yes, a chance. Tell them you went crazy. You didn't know what you were doing. There always is a chance with a good lawyer and a jury of twelve men. It's better than dead."

"How do you know, McCoy? You've never been dead."

"True, but the dead people I've seen don't look like they are having one hell of a good time." Neither of them spoke for a moment.

"You know anybody who died?" Spur asked.

"Yes! That shit-assed little boy on the stage. He pulled my mask down. The robberies were just exciting games for the four of us. Hell, we made a few dollars and nobody got hurt."

"What about the mail that didn't get delivered?"

"That's all in my dresser out at the ranch.

Hey! I wouldn't mess around with the U.S. mail! Man can get in trouble doing that!"

"Come on out, Cain. It's over. The game is over. Time to pay up on your bet. You bet and you lost, now you pay. Simple."

"Yeah, right. True. Only when they collect they stretch my neck. I'm not that crazy. I kill you and I can get out and away."

"What about the rest of the posse? They are right behind me, exxept for Efrem Longley. You hit him in the thigh, hurt him bad."

"Good! Longley caused all our trouble!"

"Not so, Cain. You caused all of your trouble. We know you were with them at the stage. You, Jim Darlow, Zack Kinsey, and Roger Olsen. We know you went crazy and killed everybody, even the horses. Why the horses, Cain?"

"They saw me. They heard my name. They could have testified against me too. I had to kill them."

"I understand."

Spur knew where he was now, at the entrance to the middle tunnel. Spur eased away from his spot and moved around the circle putting the ore car between him and Cain. The other man couldn't see Spur move.

"So, throw out your pistol, Cain. I think you're out of ammunition anyway. You never were much good with guns."

The answer came with three shots, thundering into the cavern. When the sound soaked into the rocks, Spur heard the six-gun being triggered again and again, but each time the firing pin fell on a used chamber.

Spur peered over the ore car. Cain lay in the mouth of the tunnel, looking out, pulling the trigger at regular intervals, with the weapon clicking. Spur darted around the car and jumped on top of the fugitive.

Cain dropped his gun, laughed at Spur and picked up a second pistol Spur didn't know he had. He aimed it at Spur who had holstered his own weapon.

"Now, you're going to find out how much fun it is to be dead, Spur McCoy, United States Secret Service Agent. My friends tell me it ain't no fun at all."

Spur's hand cased toward his own leather.

"Don't move it another inch, and get off me. Sit up in the dirt, then lay down, face down, right there."

Spur had no choice. He lay down. Cain reached in carefully and snatched the Peacemaker from the leather and laughed. He threw away the weapon he had been holding on Spur.

"It was empty!" Cain said. He laughed, howling in a wild kind of joy that consumed him. Spur jumped up but heard the laughter cut off and the muzzle of his own six-gun press against his forehead.

"Down, boy, down!"

Cain sat in the dirt across the six foot tunnel from Spur and stared at him. "Hell, guess you ain't such a bad sort. I just don't take to you. Don't matter. We'll both be dead in sight of twenty four hours. That is if them posse guys is any good back there."

He laughed, looked at the eagles carved into the mother-of-pearl grips on the Peacemaker. "Damn nice. Yeah, lawman. Yeah, I killed them, I had to. They would have told on me and my old pappy would have beat hell out of me. So I shot them all. I had to. I'll show you just how I did it."

He aimed the .45 at Spur and then said, "Pow, pow!" Cain laughed. Then he began to cry. Spur edged forward. Cain didn't seem to notice. Spur moved another foot.

"I see you coming," Cain said. "Shit, I can't do nothing right! Maybe this will be right!"

Cain Haworth put the muzzle of the .45 in his mouth and pulled the trigger. The big .45 slug bored through the roof of his mouth, stormed through his shattered brain and burst out of the top of his skull peeling back a four-inch chunk of bone and brains and splattered them against the top of the tunnel.

A half hour later, Spur McCoy sat outisde the old mine. Sheriff Quigley had sent two deputies into the tunnel to bring out the body. As they waited the sheriff checked Spur's wounded chest.

"Least it isn't bleeding anymore. Doc Varner's going to chew you out right good when we get back."

"I guess. How is Longley?"

"We patched him up, and told him we'd have Doc Varner come by first thing tomorrow. He'll be good as new in a month."

The sheriff waited with Spur, then looked at him. "Did Cain kill that rancher back a few miles?"

"Claims he did. I heard a shot."

"Widow said he did. She wants to thank you for . . ."

Spur waved. "She's got problems enough."

"The boys helped her bury her man. She'll be going into town until she can get some help."

Spur nodded and found that he almost went to sleep before he could stop.

When the deputies came out of the mine they put the body down and one told the sheriff they couldn't find the top of his skull.

Sheriff Quigley shook his head. "Don't matter, tie him on a horse and let's get moving. I'd just as soon walk anyway, and we're going to be at least one horse short."

Spur McCoy went to sleep three times as they rode slowly back to the Longely ranch. Efrem wouldn't let Spur leave.

"I need that man around here," Longley kept saying. He waved at his eldest daughter. "Go talk some sense into Spur."

Bee tried, but Spur could barely understand her. He let her kiss his cheek, then they rode again for town, and a bed and Spur hoped for at least twenty-four hours of sleep.

# Chapter Nineteen

Someone pounded on Spur McCoy's hotel room door at ten A.M. but he mumbled something and went back to sleep.

Doc Varner arrived about four that afternoon to inquire about his chest wound and Spur told him to go feed himself some pills.

At eight P.M., twenty-six hours after he took to his bed, Spur's feet hit the floor. He couldn't sleep anymore.

Now all he wanted was food. In the lobby he found Bee Longley waiting for him. She had been there all day. She smiled at him and his three days growth of beard, his unkempt hair and the wrinkled clothes he hadn't bothered to change after sleeping in them.

"You're beautiful!" she said.

Spur blinked. He should know who she was. Slowly the image of upthrust, hot bare breasts and pumping hips came back to him and he nodded.

"Bee . . ."

"I bet you're hungry. I tried to take you dinner once, and you threw me out. I never got into your room but you shouted some terrible things at me through the door. I think you were alseep all the time. I know you sure were mad."

He nodded and walked into the dining room. She smiled and trailed after him.

Spur sat down at a table, waved for a whole pot of coffee and drank two cups down without more than blinking at Bee who sat opposite him.

When the second cup of coffee hit bottom, he shook his head, wiped the stringy hair out of his eyes, found a comb in his pocket and combed it back, then he wiped his eyes with the white cloth napkin he had been given, and realized he wasn't really blind. He blinked the film away from his eyes and saw Bee smiling at him.

"Gorgeous!" he said, feeling the first pangs of humanity. He waved at the young girl who came to wait on him. "Just bring me some of everything, a big steak, and potatoes and half a loaf of bread and a quart of milk, lots of vegetables, and chicken if you have any. Oh, got any roasts or stew?" The girl grinned and ran for the kitchen.

Spur turned back to Bee. He sighed, shook his head again and put his chin on his fists. "Little Bee. How is your father?"

"Doc Varner said he'll live. The bullet went clean through his leg, missed the bone. I tied it up tight so he didn't lose too much blood. I . . . I never got a chance to thank you for saving my life."

"He wouldn't have killed you."

"He would . . . afterward. He told me that. Said how good I was depended how long I lived. He wasn't a nice man."

"No."

"Have you seen Doc yet?"

"No."

"I'll go find him and have him come see you just as soon as you finish eating!" She was up and gone before he could protest. Spur had another cup of coffee and the fried chicken and roast and potatoes and brown gravy and vegetables came. There were six dishes with food on larger than normal plates. The waitress said his steak was coming, did he want it seared on the outside and raw in the middle as usual? He nodded and went back to eating.

Sheriff Quigley stopped by at his table.

"Rip Van Winkle, you woke up."

"Nearly."

"Before you go to sleep again, how do you want me to charge the two surviving stage coach robbers?"

"With stage robbery. Olsen gets a break on his sentence if he gives evidence against Darlow and pleads guilty."

"And the two arsonists?"

"How did Haworth take the confession and suicide of his son?"

"Hard. Lot and Abel had to help him walk to the funeral this morning. He's aged twenty years this week. Abel says he's running the ranch now. He's assured me he'll pay for materials to rebuild the barns at the two ranches, and that there won't be any more trouble."

"Let's charge the two arsonists with arson, stiffest kind possible according to Wyoming Territorial law, and forget about Henry Haworth. He's paid enough." Spur paused and cut a big chunk off the two-inch thick T-Bone steak. "That is unless you want to handle the cases some other way. This is your primary jurisdiction."

"No, no I like your suggestion. I'll get the papers drawn up in the morning. If you stop by I do have some other papers I need you to sign. Concerning the suicide, the confession, and the death of the rancher."

"Right. About ten or eleven. I may sleep in again."

"Don't blame you." Quigley watched Spur finish another drumstick and break a huge piece of bread off the loaf. "Are you sure you're getting enough to eat? I understand they have some great apple pie here served with a wedge of the sharpest cheese in the country."

Spur nodded. "Good. I hadn't even thought of dessert."

When he finished the food, he felt ten pounds heavier, but the great chalky empty spot in his chest had been filled and he felt better. He headed back upstairs, noticing his clothes for the first time. He could also use a bath.

The moment he came into his room he saw Bee testing a tub of bathwater. Steam rose from a bucket of hot water beside the tub. A chair held two towels and a bar of soap.

"I . . . I thought you might want a nice relaxing bath."

"Sounds good."

"I get to wash you."

Spur smiled. "That also sounds good. But what would your daddy say?"

"He already has approved. When us Longleys want something, we go after it. I told him I was going to hound you until you married me, even if I had to bed you first."

Spur chuckled. "I bet he swatted you for that."

"No, he just looked me up and down, and said to go to it. He said if I couldn't do it, then it couldn't be done . . . get you to tie the knot."

"Sounds like a challenge."

"It will be fun to try." She began unbuttoning his shirt, and he caught her hands and kissed her, then let her continue.

A short time later Spur settled in the tub, his knees sticking out. It felt good to get a backscrub again. She was careful not to get the bandage wet.

"Doc Varner was out at a ranch welcoming a baby to the world. His wife said you should come see him tomorrow."

Spur nodded. Bee was still fully dressed. She had hardly hesitated when she pulled his pants and under drawers off, but now as she washed lower and lower he saw her begin to get excited.

"Should I wash . . . everything?" she asked. Spur nodded.

"Oh!" She frowned. "Then, you'll have to stand up."

Spur did and she giggled as she soaped his flaccid penis and his heavy scrotum. She washed his legs quickly and came back to his crotch.

"You figure there's any way we could get him to take a little interest in the bath giver?" Spur asked.

"We could try," she said flashing him a smile. Quickly she washed the soap off his crotch then reached in and held him and kissed the limp head. She yelped as it pulsed and lifted slightly. She laughed and kissed it again, then fondled him and in a minute he was straight and bold and hard.

"Now that is more like it!" Bee said. She unbuttoned her dress and opened the bodice. Bee caught his hand and put it inside the opening and under her chemise.

"My that feels good!" she said. "All kind of warm and soft, and . . . just nice!"

Spur stepped from the tub and picked her up, holding her fast to his still wet body and carried her to the bed.

"So you told your old dad you might bed me did you?"

"I told you, I go after what I want!"

He dropped her on the bed and sat down

beside her.

"Fair is fair. We had a fling a few days ago, right? No promises, no strings, no demands."

"Yes, and it was beautiful."

"So I must be fair with you. I can't marry you. I can't stay here. I can't take you with me. I'm a roving man, that's my job. I'm in a different town almost every week. I'm not the man for you."

Bee bit her lip. "And . . . and my letting you have me all night isn't going to change your mind?"

"Right. That's what I'm telling you. A girl has to think about her reputation."

Tears squeezed out of protesting eyelids. "Damnit! I want you so bad! Why can't it be different?"

"It will be for you, some day, with someone. Now, before I touch you again, you can button up your dress and comb your hair and get in the buggy and I'll have a reliable man drive you back to your ranch, or you can go stay overnight with Betty and her parents."

"Oh, damn!" She sat up and leaned in and kissed him hard, then she bounced off the bed and quickly lifted the dress over her head, then three petticoats until she had on only a thin chemise and her knee length drawers.

"No. I want to stay here with you . . . all night, if you'll have me. I want to make love with you a dozen times, and have you show me all the tender ways to love a man and tell you how I feel and I want you to tell me how you feel and pretend just for one night that I am married to you." She stopped and sat on his lap and kissed his lips hungrily. She watched him closely for his reaction.

He nodded.

Her face blossomed with a beautiful smile, the frown gone.

"Then if I never do meet that perfect man and love and marry him, I'll have a powerful memory to help me get through the days, and I can always dream about what might have been."

She pushed back off his lap into the bed, and lifted the chemise over her head and lay there waiting.

Spur lay beside her, leaned over her and kissed both her breasts and smiled down at her. "Bathsheba Longley, you are one hell of a lot of woman. You are young and eager and so sexy it makes me leap to attention. I'm passing up a beautiful woman here by not taking you with me. But it just couldn't work."

She sighed. "You know for sure, because you've had this same problem before."

"Somewhat the same. But never such a beautiful, beguiling, sexy, marvelous problem."

She blinked rapidly and a single tear seeped out of one eye and ran down her cheek.

"You know just the right thing to say. Now quickly make love to me gently and all night and let me fill up a storehouse of sweet memories to last as long as I need them."

He kissed her and lay gently over her.

"Bee, I'm going to have a stack of wonderful memories to keep me going, too."

It began gently, with soft, tender passion, and before it was over the first time had grown into a furious, fire-filled rampage of every emotion they had ever felt, and ended with a clawing, scratching, wailing pair of climaxes that came together in a performance they knew would be hard to top. But they would try.

They had nothing to eat or drink in the room, and by the time he thought of it, it was too late. For a while they sat side by side on the bed, talking quietly. She poured her soul out to him, telling him her deepest secrets, things she had never told anyone. She told him how Betty had played with her one night in bed and they both had become excited and rubbed each other into climaxes.

"Since then I do it myself once in a while. Is that so bad?"

"It's not bad at all. But a man should excite you more than that ever could."

Bee grinned and played with his limp lance.

"There is no problem there! I am simply floored by the way you get me so worked up I want to lay on my back for you. Will it be that way with me for some other man?"

"Yes. Making love, having sex, is a natural act. Mother Nature intended it that way. Everyone is good at sex, it's like saying someone is good at breathing. We all can do it. Sex is the same way. The trick is to find the right person to be with, to love, to marry."

"Oh, I know, and I thought I had!"

"But it has to be right for BOTH people."

"Yes, now I understand." She hesitated. "Would it hurt, I mean would it be all right if I was on top?"

Spur laughed and pulled her on top of him "No hurt of mine can be so bad that you can't lay on top of it." He grinned. "Especially when you are all beautiful and naked and sexy this way."

They made love again, gently and they talked all the time, telling each other exactly how they felt, when the thrill came and how it felt, every tingle and breathlessness, every spasm and climax.

They slept after that and woke early in the morning before dawn for one last lingering lovemaking as the day began.

Spur sat on the edge of the bed and watched her dress.

"Will I ever see you again?"

"My business here will be done soon." He stopped and frowned, walked to the window and looked out the blind. A soft rain fell outside. The heavy clouds looked loaded with water vapor.

"It's raining!" he said.

"Oh, wonderful!"

"Looks like it's going to rain all day and all night, a real soaker. The drought may be over."

"See what wonderful luck you've brought us? Sure you won't stay? I've got a big ranch to offer you, and me." She threw her arms wide and pushed her breasts out.

Spur kissed her cheek and managed to miss the tub of bath water which still sat in the middle of the room.

"I think you better wait for a better offer. One of these days somebody around here is going to knock your socks off. Have you ever said hello to Lot or Abel Haworth?"

"Not on your life!"

"Things are going to be different now. Both are extremely fine young men. Make it a point to say hello the next time you 'just happen' to walk past them. It could prove interesting. And what a joint venture the two biggest ranches would make!"

A small smile began to play in Bee's eyes and around her delicate mouth as she thought about the handsome Haworth boys.

Spur kissed her mouth, then walked her to his door. She reached up and kissed him once more, then tied her sunbonnet on and headed for the desk to find out where they had put her buggy.

Spur smiled as the door shut. Then he dove back in bed and pulled the covers up over his head. Now maybe he could catch up on some of his sleep before he confronted Dr. Varner. Then the sheriff and finally Claudine over at the Pink Petticoat.

# Chapter Twenty

Spur spent a half hour shaving, combing his hair and dressing. He put on his black suit, ruffled front white shirt with the big cufflinks, and a narrow string tie, then went to see Doc Varner. The sawbones pretended he didn't know him. At last he stared at Spur and scowled.

"Sonny, next time I tell you to stay in bed three days after you been shot up bad, you damn well stay in bed!"

"Yes sir," Spur said.

Doc grinned. "Damn glad you didn't this time. Most of the town was shocked by what Cain Haworth done. Everybody knew he was a little wild, but had no idea he was that crazy. Just never can tell about people. Me, I'm going into veterinary medicine. Patients never backtalk you."

"You want to take a look at me or not?" Spur said with an easy irreverence.

"Might as well now that you wasted this much of my time. Didn't have to dress up formal just to come see me."

"I always do."

Five minutes later, Doc Varner had the

wound examined, put on some more of his favorite ointment and wrapped it tightly again.

"I'd guess you're getting ready to travel. That bandage will do for a week, less you get too active. Healing up fine. Bother you any?"

"Only when I lose a wrestling match with a pretty woman."

"Serves you right."

Spur gave the doctor a twenty dollar gold piece. "That take care of my bill?"

"And then some."

"Put it down for one of your charity cases."

"Done." Doc looked up. "Where you heading from here?"

"To a telegraph to find out what kind of orders, directives and problems I have. It's a big country."

"True. And I think I've got twins coming. If I can tear myself away from your sparkling wit and conversation."

Spur laughed, waved goodbye and went out the door heading for the sheriff's office.

Sheriff Quigley was in and waiting. He had the papers all drawn up in his secretary's best printing waiting for Spur's signature. Two were complaints, two sets of charges, and an account of how Cain had shot himself as Spur had told it to the sheriff. Spur made one small change and signed it. The last document dealt with the death of the rancher who had been shot by Cain. Spur signed it as well.

"Ever find the rest of the double gold

eagles that belong to Marshall Sullivan over at the bank?" Spur asked.

"All of them but one. Cain had a hundred of them in that same drawer with the mail. A lot of folks are breathing easier now that the mail has been delivered. All sorts of important papers in those packs. At least that boy didn't burn the mail."

"Small favors," Spur said. There was nothing else to be said. Spur reminded the sheriff he wouldn't be around for the trials, but they had more than enough evidence to convict all four men on the arson and robbery charges.

"Stop by and see us anytime," Sheriff Quigley said.

"Don't wait up for me," Spur said, grinned and walked out the door.

Next stop for Spur was the Pink Petticoat. He waved at Barry behind the bar and went back to Claudine's private quarters. He knocked and then opened the door. She sat at her little kitchen table with a long black cigar in her mouth and a cup of coffee beside her.

"Don't say a word," Spur said. "I'm basking in the glory of being your local hero, and now I want a little peace and quiet and some slow easy loving as I recuperate for a few days from being shot, trampled and put upon."

Claudine chuckled softly and waved her hand toward the bedroom.

"Yes, oh lord and master, what would you desire first?"

"A little rest, a bunch of good food and a lot of loving."

"In that order?"

"In any damn order you want," he said. He was tired. Suddenly tired of running and watching over his shoulder. Tired of being shot at and punched and kicked and trampled and always having to be right.

Claudine would understand. She would put up with his guff for a few days. It was a reaction. He often got this way after a tough case. It passed. At least so far it had. He sat down and pointed to her coffee cup. She poured and he realized he hadn't had any breakfast.

"Food," he said, and bent over, putting his head on his crossed arms on the table. He relaxed and was asleep. As he slept the dream came again, the dream of someone chasing him, and he wasn't sure if they would catch him or not. Just as the evil looking man with the big gun closed in on him, someone shook his shoulder.

"Bacon and eggs, hashbrown potatoes, fresh biscuits, coffee and blackberry jam. Will that do?"

Spur came out of the dream and grinned.

"Yeah, that's going to do. Just don't tell anyone where I'm at, not for at least three days."

Spur began eating his breakfast and Claudine watched him, a patient, knowing expression on her face as the tip of her tongue moistened her lips.